PROVOKE ME

THE LAST VOCARI: BOOK 2

ELENA LAWSON

This is a work of fiction. Characters, incidents and dialogs are products of the author's
imagination and are not to be construed as real. Any resemblance to actual events is strictly
coincidental.
Cover by Moorbooks Design

1

I wanted to rip his fucking head off.

It was damn near impossible to hide the swell of thoughts the moment I looked into his eyes. Like a dam lowering, they flowed unrestrained into the forefront of my mind.

It's him.

Holy fucking shit it's him…

The bastard who murdered *my mother.*

Right here. Right now. Trying to cut a motherfucking deal *with me.*

I quelled the urge to charge him with shaking fingers. Had to snuff out the burning thoughts so he wouldn't hear them. Hot, furious tears welled along the rims of my eyes, and I lowered my head, not wanting him to see. My teeth clenched together so hard I thought I'd crack a damned tooth.

He must have kept his word this time. He

must've been staying out of my thoughts because he said nothing, just waited there patiently for my response.

My response?

Right—he'd asked me a question I had yet to answer.

"Do we have an agreement?" the vampire called Azrael asked again, repeating the question more slowly, as though he were speaking to a young child.

My skin bristled at the barely concealed condescension and disgust in his tone. My heart thundered in my ears and I made a knee-jerk decision. "Yes," I ground out.

"Good."

He rose from the chair by the fireplace with practiced grace. I didn't dare look up again—still trying to conceal my thoughts from him.

I imagined a blank wall of white stone in my mind and focused on building it larger to try to stop the hemorrhaging of thoughts I was trying to conceal.

The ancient vampire went to move away, and my heart skittered. I glanced around at my surroundings; the cold stone walls, the bed, a side table, and the open maw of the hearth were the only things in the congested space. My stomach dropped. He was *not* about to leave me here in this fucking *tomb*.

"Wait," I stopped him, my face pinching with the effort of keeping my voice level. "Where am I?"

He didn't reply.

"How long do I have to stay here?"

Still no reply. The fucker left me staring at his back. His long russet hair glinting with strands of red in the firelight. His thick shoulders tensing with each question I asked.

I gulped, deciding to change tactics. It was obvious I was stuck here—at least for now. But there was one thing I needed from him before I could condemn myself to this cold cell. One small bit of reassurance.

"I want to see that they're alright." I tried to sound demanding, but as my hands curled into fists in the fur atop the bed, I only managed to sound pathetic to my own ears.

"And you shall," Azrael responded, his deep voice gravelly. "Once you've proven…*cooperative* with my requests."

I stiffened.

"Rest now, sweet Rose. I'll have someone bring you something to eat shortly. You'll be needing your strength."

When I looked up, he was gone. A whisper of movement the only indication he'd been there at all.

Fuck.

I smashed my fist against the bedpost and growled my frustration, the pain of my knuckles splitting open against the hard wood helping to sharpen my focus. Warm blood dribbled down my fingers as I shook out the sting.

The deluge of thoughts came back as the white stone wall I'd erected around them fell flat. I could only pray Azrael was far enough away that he wouldn't hear them.

Angry as I was that he wouldn't allow me to see the guys—to verify with my own eyes that they were unscathed—a slow smile spread across my lips and I shivered at the intense feeling of anticipation that washed over me like a balm to my shaken nerves.

Reeling back, I hit the bedpost again and was rewarded with the beautiful sound of splitting wood as the top section of the post broke off from the base and skipped onto the bed and clattered to the floor. The sharp edge where it'd broken free from the whole wouldn't need much whittling to be shaped into a stake.

'I'd encountered this phenomenon only once before, but unfortunately the subject died…'

Azrael had all but told me from his own lips that he was the one who'd murdered her. And his eyes were proof enough for me. They were the same ones I'd hunted for the last ten years. The ones I checked for after each kill—hopeful that I'd finally delivered the true death to the one who ended the life of the only family I had left.

I'd play this fucker's little game.

He wanted a cooperative captive and I'd give him one.

Azrael was clearly the oldest vampire I'd ever encountered. He'd be the fastest and the strongest too. I had no doubt. I could feel it in my bones whenever he drew near. That *otherness* made my blood buzz and my heart pound in warning against the monster it sensed before it.

I wasn't naïve enough to think I could take him with nothing but a wooden stake and pure rage.

I would need to heal and gather my strength. To get a lay of this creepy ass cave he had me trapped in.

It would take time and careful planning.

It would take patience.

But I smiled because The Black Rose *never* lost. I was infamous for a reason. *There was a bounty on my head for a reason.* Azrael knew my name because the underground world of immortal beasts whispered it in hushed tones, afraid to speak it too loudly for fear of conjuring me.

I smiled as I ran the edge of the busted bedpost back and forth against the rough stone floor because…Azrael had just given me my greatest challenge yet.

2

Azrael wasn't lying about sending someone in with food. A slight woman with graying hair in a tight bun and a soft and warm countenance came into my room about an hour later.

By then I'd had time to sufficiently destroy the rest of the bed frame and posts and completely shatter the small end table to unrecognizable bits against the stone floor. My newly fashioned stake was carefully tucked up into the bottom of the bedframe, and with all the destruction, I hoped no one would be able to tell there was a piece missing.

Though if this Azrael fucker had lived as long as I assumed he had, I had to believe it wasn't because he was stupid. But *cocky* was another form of stupid I'd found most males with half a brain possessed. Azrael may catch on to the fact that I planned to kill him—he just had to be cocky enough to believe I posed no threat. Then I could prove otherwise.

"*Oh!*" The older woman exclaimed as she entered my chamber from the dark stone hall. A hall I fully intended to investigate as soon as I was able to re-break and set the bones in my foot.

The woman huffed, and I felt for the otherness that would tell me whether she was a vampire but felt nothing. She couldn't have been more than five feet tall and at least fifty—she posed no threat—even in my current state. But that didn't stop me from watching her every movement like a hawk circling prey.

I didn't make it as far as I had in life by underestimating people.

"This won't do," she tutted as she set the tray down on the bed next to me, clucking her tongue. My mouth watered at the feast laid out on the tray. A thick and juicy-looking steak, herbed potatoes, and buttered green beans. The white mug was steaming with an aroma that could only be coffee, and a tall glass pitcher of water dominated one side of the tray.

I swallowed hard, hesitating to reach out for the water. What if it was poisoned? What if it was all poisoned?

"Master Azrael is going to be *so* upset…"

The woman bent to begin cleaning the mess on

the floor, tossing small pieces of wood into the fire. It was like I wasn't even here.

"Uh..." I began, watching as she knelt among the mess, gathering her apron and skirts to sit back on her heels. "I'm...sorry?" I tried, the word souring on my tongue.

If I was going to have any chance of getting what I wanted, I had to at least pretend to be pliant. To '*cooperate*' as Azrael said.

She finally looked up and her glassy faded blue eyes roved over me. She clucked her tongue again and shook her head. "You're *skin and bones*. Go on—eat up and then I'll take you to the devil's spring."

"The *what*?"

"To *bathe*," she threw her hands up and huffed as though it were the most obvious thing in the world. "Begging your pardon, miss, but you look positively awful. I've never seen a grown adult so dirty."

She was going to take me out of this cell?

My eyes widened as a thought struck me and I shoved myself from the bed and knelt in front of her at eye level. She recoiled back in surprise, but then her gaze met mine.

I let the power of my compulsion rise within me and focused my thoughts on twisting hers. "Show me the way out of here," I said.

She blinked twice and cocked her head at me. "I can't, dear. I'm afraid I don't know it, myself."

Groaning, I rocked back on my heels, biting the inside of my cheek as I considered another route. When I glanced back up at her, I found her watching me curiously and I realized all at once that the glassiness I saw in her eyes wasn't the dull gloss of age, but the shining veneer of compulsion.

Fuck.

She'd already been compelled. And if it was Azrael who compelled her, there was no way in hell my compulsion would be strong enough to combat his.

Solemnly, I bowed my head. "Never mind," I said and hobbled back to the bed on my broken foot, grimacing.

The woman continued clearing the mess from the floor, muttering something to herself. She was old enough to be a mother—maybe even a grandmother. I wondered what family the beast had snatched her away from and a bolt of sizzling fury rippled through my body.

What right did he have to kidnap people and bend them to his will? I tried to get a look at her neck beneath the collar of her blouse but couldn't tell whether or not there were puncture marks there. If he was feeding on her, too, I might just vomit.

"Eat, girl!" The woman chastised as she rose, adjusting her back to get out an obvious crick. "You're skin and bones."

My mouth watered again as I looked down at

the tray. For half a second, I thought eating it would be worth the risk of poisoning…

"Do you think the master's poisoned it?" The woman asked, seemingly confused at my reaction.

I didn't answer, just glared down at my steak and potatoes.

"Foolish girl!"

She stomped over to the bed and plucked a potato from the tray, popping it in her mouth. "The master wouldn't dream to feed you *poison.* How ridiculous," she said around the mouthful of potato. "I didn't spend my evening for it to go to waste. If you won't have it, *I* will."

As she swallowed the hunk of root veg, I watched her carefully, making sure there were no obvious signs of poisoning.

Finally, she huffed and threw up her hands. "Starve, then, if you please," she balked, and turned to leave. "I'll be back to take you for bathing just as soon as I'm finished with the mess in the kitchen."

I considered the food in front of me again, and a thought crossed my mind—prodded by something she'd said. *'The master wouldn't dream to feed you poison…'*

He said he needed me, hadn't he? This *Azrael* needed me to cooperate. And I couldn't very well do that if I were dead or ill from poisoning, could I?

Begrudgingly, I knelt before the tray, my mouth watering as I carved a massive bite from the steak with the dull butter knife I was given in lieu of a proper steak knife. *Smart fuckers.* Though, it didn't seem to matter much. The meat was incredibly tender and came apart easily under the pressure of the knife.

I didn't stop at the first bite. Suddenly ravenous and eager for my body to finish healing itself, I'd inhaled the entire meal within ten minutes. Finished all the water, too.

Distantly, I felt the weak urge to use a bathroom, but with my stomach full and the adrenaline of waking in a strange place, with a strange man, fading…I found it almost impossible to keep my eyes open.

Had I been wrong?

Was the food laced with something, after all?

A…a sleeping elixir, maybe?

My vision doubled. And then tripled. The weights on my eyelids grew heavier and my head spun as I flopped back onto the fur and cushions.

3

His hands circled my thighs, gripping tightly to the supple flesh there as he pulled my legs apart. My heart skittered into a frenzied pounding in my chest as his warm breath gently caressed my lips.

I was buck ass naked and tied to the bed like before, except this time there was no blindfold. My hands were tightly bound with leather straps to the bed posts, and my legs were tied the same, but with a little more slack in the length of stiff leather cord.

Between my legs was Blake. I could just make him out in the flickering light of the fire. The roaring flames in the old stone hearth making his near-black hair shine with red fire and his dark eyes flash every time he looked up at me.

"Blake," I whimpered, pulling at the binds holding me against the mattress. I wanted to run my fingers through his hair. I wanted to trace the lines of every whorl of black ink on his immaculate body. I wanted to kiss every fucking inch of him. And then I wanted to take the proud length of him into my mouth and let the little minx in the back of my mind take over until he saw stars and nothing else.

I could do none of those things. Not tied up like I was. I was powerless to do anything but writhe and moan as he finally *mercifully* took my pussy into his mouth, his expert tongue circling my clit.

Fuck.

He really knew what he was doing down there, another few minutes and this Rose would burst into a puddle of petals against the satin sheets.

I arched my back as he slipped two fingers inside, playing me like a musical instrument. I hissed and moaned and nearly screamed when he started that maddening flicking with his tongue again.

"Come for me, Rose," he paused to whisper against the sensitive flesh and something inside me came undone at the commanding tone in his voice. He wasn't asking me. It was an order. And my body felt the need to *obey*.

I came against his lips, as his fingers drove into me again and again, lengthening the orgasm until all my muscles were coiled tight and bright spots crowded my vision.

I didn't have the chance to get my head straight or to clear my vision before Blake had moved. My body heaved and my breath left me in a great gasping breath as he *impaled* my pussy. The thrust so hard it was almost painful, but the *almost pain* made the pleasure that much more delicious.

Blake settled himself inside of me and I looked up to find my tall-dark-and-handsome staring down at me with a delicious grin on his lips. I bit my lip at the marvel of him and he growled, his fangs sliding low. My heart pumped and my blood sang with the need for him to bite me.

I wanted those fangs inside of me just as surely as I wanted his cock.

I bared my neck to him, and he hissed, sliding himself out only to drive back in *hard*—a punishment for tempting him. As Blake began to circle his hips slowly, letting me adjust to the size of him while simultaneously hitting *every fucking nerve* down there, my body shook with desire and longing. Greedy and wanting another release already.

"Not yet," Blake commanded. "You'll cum when I say so."

I nodded, straining against my binds as he began pumping into me, slowly at first, but then faster, and faster still, until I was on the verge and the ability to contain myself was slipping.

"Good girl," he said, his own voice straining now.

His cock drove into me again and again, and as my eyelids fluttered open, I saw how his fangs were out in earnest now and my body responded to the desire, my back arching up sharply until he couldn't stop himself.

Blake's head lowered until my breast was in his mouth, until his fangs pierced the sensitive skin there. I cried out at the initial pain, but as the pain smoothed out into an intense and all-consuming pleasure radiating out through every nerve, I shivered. Blake drank from me as he fucked me until I could hardly see for all the sensations taking over my mind and body.

I was a mass of senses. Of touch and smell and pain and pleasure and strain and *pressure* as his thrusts became harder and quicker, him close to finding his own release, too.

Fuck, I couldn't hold on any longer, I couldn't contain it. It was like trying to stop a bullet midair. Impossible.

Blake's fangs slid free of my skin and he growled, "*Now, baby*."

I shattered in a million tiny pieces as the force of the orgasm hit me like a fucking hurricane, swirling and wet and *hot* as hell. My body clenched around Blake as he found his own release, cumming into me with a broken moan of his own.

"Oh, good, you're awake."

I sat bolt upright at the sudden sound of a voice ringing against stone. It took me a moment to come out of the fevered dream, still breathing hard with an ache between my thighs. A profound sadness settled over me like a leaden weight when reality set it. Blake wasn't here. None of the guys were. I was all alone.

The woman from before bustled into the stone chamber, a white towel and what looked to be a dark purple bathrobe folded in her arms.

"Up you get, girl. The master will be wanting to see you before the night is through."

Still nighttime, then? So, I hadn't been asleep long. I wondered how in the world she could tell what time it was. I didn't see a watch on her wrist, and other than the low glow of embers in the hearth, there wasn't a lick of natural light to be seen.

Trying to get my bearings with a shake of my head and a deep breath, I slunk from the bed, testing my broken foot softly against the cool floor. *Nope.* Wouldn't be walking on that until I could set it. I cursed under my breath. Why couldn't it have been a dislocated shoulder, or a broken arm? I'd managed to re-set those before without much issue.

But a foot? I'd never broken it before, and I knew enough about bones to know that there were too many in my foot for me to be able to set it properly without some help. I would try, but I shivered to think of how many times I'd have to break and reset it before I got it right enough to walk on.

The woman didn't seem to care at all that I

could barely walk, she vanished into the shadow of the corridor, leaving me grunting, clutching the wall for support as I hopped to follow her as quickly as I could.

We wove a long path through the labyrinthine underground dwelling. I thought it must be some sort of cave. The walls were rough stone, and there didn't seem to be any form of electricity. Flaming torches lined the walkways every so often, but not nearly close together enough to be able to see everything.

The spaces between the torches were pitch black and, in those spaces, I had only the steady footfalls of the woman in front of me to direct me. I felt more than one opening in the stone—almost fucking *fell into one of them*—on the way to this so-called *devil's spring*. The network of tunnels seemed endless, and much as I tried to memorize the route we were taking, I lost the pattern after the eleventh turn.

This was going to take longer than I thought. I ground my teeth, checking to make sure the butter knife I'd tucked into the waistband of my skirt was still there. It was. I patted it, reminding myself that I didn't need a sharp object as a weapon. I'd taken down a vampire with a *spoon*. A butter knife would prove a much better defense.

Though, judging by the tepid silence within the

suffocated stone walls, I was beginning to think we were the only people down here.

The scent of sulfur was the first sign we were drawing nearer to the spring. And within a few seconds more I could faintly hear the trickle of water over stone and the echoing *shhhh* of a small waterfall somewhere underground.

"Here we are," The woman proclaimed as the tunnel opened into a wide dark chamber filled with steam that tickled at the back of my throat with the strong tang of minerals. It was *hot* inside the room, and I squinted to be able to see better by the light of the single, low-burning torch set into the wall next to the entrance.

I could make out the surface of the water in the cave—looking like no more than an undulating floor of shadows carved into the hard rock. The steam made it difficult to decipher where the rock ended, and the water began.

There was something else here, too. A prickle along the back of my neck alerted me to the fact we weren't alone. I shivered even though I was warmer than I'd been since I'd awoken in this hellish place. I knew that feeling.

Azrael's particular brand of vampire was easy to decipher. The atmospheric weight of his presence was so great it settled like a weight on my chest—crushing me.

"Well, I'll leave you to it," the woman said as she

bent to set the towel and bathrobe down on a hewn stone bench a few feet away from the entrance. "Back to get you in a bit. Don't try to go anywhere by yourself, girl. This place has swallowed up more than its fair share of wandering souls with its intricate pathways. Would hate to see you fall prey to it, too."

I barely heard her, I was staring out into the black water, searching for him.

"Did you hear me?"

"Hmm?" I said, snapping back to myself.

The woman threw her hands up and turned away to leave. "Just stay put until I come back."

"That won't be necessary."

His voice floated out from the dark recesses of the cave—and from the distance, I had to guess the spring was a lot larger and went a lot further into the dark than I originally thought.

"Oh! Master Azrael. I'm so sorry. I didn't know you were bathing, sir," the woman's hand curled around my upper arm and began dragging me back the way we'd come. "I'll bring the girl back later, sir. So sorry for disturb—"

"Leave her, Estelle. I can smell her stench from here."

I bristled, cheeks inflaming with an emotion that burned hotter than embarrassment. The only reason I stank was because he'd fucking kidnapped me and left me in a bed covered in blood and sweat.

"But, sir?"

"I'll escort her back to her chamber once she's finished."

I still couldn't see him in the darkness at the other end of the cavern, and my jaw twitched, and stomach soured at the thought of being left alone with him again. At the thought of *bathing* with the monster who—

I shut down the thought, clamping my jaw tightly as I began to erect that white wall of stone in my mind again. I had no idea if it was helping, but it was worth a shot.

"Yes, sir, as you say. I'll be going then."

She released me and I saw a flicker of something like worry in her glassy gaze before she straightened her spine and released me, disappearing into the shadows, back the way we'd come.

I couldn't help how my heart raced as the echo of her footfalls faded into nothing as she drew further and further away—leaving me with the devil in the spring.

Azrael didn't speak, and I still couldn't see him. After a few minutes, I began to wonder if he was still there at all? If it weren't for the creeping feeling still making gooseflesh rise along my arms and back of my neck, I'd have assumed he'd left. The only sounds were the trickling of droplets over stone and the gentle *shhh* of a small flow of water somewhere off to my right.

"Are you just going to stand there?"

That same fury I'd felt before bubbled up again. It was impossibly difficult to contain it. I'd never really had to before.

In the game of cat and mouse I'd played with vampire kind for the last several years—I'd always been the cat.

"And now you're the mouse. How very…ironic," his voice slithered over me, and I thought it sounded closer than it had a moment before.

I gulped, cheeks aflame. "Stay *out* of my head."

He didn't answer right away, and when he did, I wasn't sure I heard him right. But it sounded like, "As you wish."

I edged closer to the rim of the pool, keeping my weight on my good foot while I swept the broken one forward to feel where the rock ended and the water began beneath the rising gray steam. Finally, after several feet of hobbling, my toes touched hot water and I shuddered at how *incredible* it felt.

I swallowed hard as I swept my gaze one last time over the spring. He would be able to see me plainly because of the flickering torchlight at my back—whereas as I couldn't see him because he was sticking to the shadows further back.

Dick.

I thought I heard a chuckle, but I couldn't be sure it wasn't just the burbling of water rising from somewhere deep below the surface.

Fuck this. I needed a goddamned bath.

Strengthening my resolve, I tore off my shirt.

My bra fell next, and then my skirt. I was careful to pull it down by the hem, holding the dull knife in the waistband with my thumb. As I scooted to the edge of the water, I turned to lower myself down, still in my panties, and when I thought my body was in position to conceal the maneuver, I released the skirt, taking the knife with me as I sank lower into the spring.

The heat swirled around me, seeping into my pores. It felt somehow heavier than normal water. And instead of just wetting me and warming, it seemed to sort of *caress* me. As though it were laced with the most luxurious of essential oils. I shivered as the chill fled my skin, and the warmth began to soak into deeper layers. Softening muscle and soothing aches I didn't even know were there.

I gripped the dull knife hard between my thighs as I tipped my head back and dipped my long hair in the water, running my fingers through it to loosen the tangles and soak out the blood and dirt.

The water came up to my chest, just above my breasts, but they bobbed in the water, floating a bit so my nipples were only just covered.

Though I wasn't one for modesty, even I had to admit, bathing in the same pool as the monster who kidnapped me was hideously uncomfortable. The disquieting feeling all the more strong because this time I knew I wasn't stronger than my foe. I didn't have a chance if he decided to attack.

But Azrael didn't make a sound and I couldn't see him through the dark haze. It made it easier to assume he was far away and would stay there until I was finished.

Removing the knife from between my legs, I limped against the slick stone floor beneath the water, feeling a source of more heat over to my left where the trickling sound was coming from. Eager to be even warmer than I was, I followed the trail of heat and the trickling noise, feeling some of the aching in my foot ease with each step. I wondered offhandedly if the water held some kind of healing properties.

A witch could have spelled it. Or enchanted it. Or whatever it was witches did. I didn't have enough experience with them to know how their magic worked.

As I drew nearer the source of the sound and the heat, I could see that I was coming up on a rock face, and when I reached out to touch it, I could feel scalding water running over a worn crevasse down into the spring. I recoiled back, shocked at how hot it was. It had to be boiling. It felt like fucking lava.

Devil's Spring, indeed.

"Quite hot, isn't it?"

My mouth parted and my eyes widen as I whirled around, blindly striking out with the butter knife. I heard a muffled grunt and an iron grip came around my wrist, holding my hand—still holding the blade—high above my head. The silver tip dripped crimson.

I grinned.

Azrael's mis-matched eyes glinted in the whisper of torchlight—making them look black in the dark, with fire in the place where his pupils should have been. My chest heaved as I drew in breath after breath, waiting with my fist clenched and stance wide for his retaliation. He tilted his head to one side, studying me.

His gaze went lower, touching the curve of my jawline. My throat and the wild pulse it contained.

Lower still. Until he was looking at the jagged scar across my neck.

My traitorous lower lip trembled as the memory of how it was made came back in a rush of pain-filled emotions. I tried to stifle it, but there it was, clear as though it'd only just happened because here he was. The monster who did it.

I'd been so small. So innocent back then.

I was fourteen again. Screaming my sorrow over my mother's prone body, my knees and hands coated in a thick layer of her blood as I sobbed uncontrollably into her chest. My body wracking with the force of my anguish. I screamed and I screamed. My chest felt as though it would burst from the sheer agony washing over me in crashing waves that made it difficult to breathe.

My small hands curled into her wool sweater.

My tears dropping like broken promises onto her cheeks.

She would never hold me again.

Her eyes wouldn't ever open.

And all the while he stood there looking down at her with something like reverence in his gaze. Like he was *proud* of his handiwork. He was admiring his *art*.

Pain-fueled hatred burned brightly behind my breastbone and adrenaline snaked through my veins like acid, burning hotter and brighter than anything I'd ever felt before.

I attacked him. My strangled sobs became an ear-splitting battle-cry as I descended upon him, hands clawed, and teeth bared. It was useless, of course.

I was a child. I had no weapon. No fighting experience save for some basic self-defense training I'd learned from Mom. I lost before I even stood up.

The vampire swung his hand in a wide arc, stopping me from even reaching him. His razor-sharp nails sliced into me as though they were a fucking buzz saw.

All I remembered before I fell to my knees was the warmth of oozing blood as it ran between my breasts and filled the cups of my bra. I could remember it being difficult to breathe. And I remembered how he'd smiled when I fell, too. His pearly white fangs gleaming under the glow of the streetlamps before he vanished in the blink of an eye and the darkness began to creep in.

I didn't realize tears were welling in my eyes until Azrael released my hand and I let it fall limply back to the water, dropping the useless piece of cutlery to sink to the bottom. I felt just as helpless in that moment as I did then.

When I looked up into the face of the monster again, I found a deep sadness etched into his eyes and the hard line of his jaw. A faraway look in his gaze.

Was he remembering what he did to us?

Was he fucking reveling in it?

I wanted him dead. I didn't care anymore if he heard my thoughts. Let him know it. I wanted to rip his motherfucking head off and I would find a way to do it.

His eyes flashed with a dangerous glint as our gazes met. A challenge?

"I *will* kill you for what you did to her," I told him, knowing he'd been listening. He'd seen his *'art'* replay in my memories. "I promise you that."

The tiniest of smiles twitched at the corner of his thick lips and my stomach pooled with dread. "You can try."

My chest ached as his unspoken admission and

a quiet understanding began to settle over my bones.

"But my brother won't be killed so easily, my sweet Rose."

"Your…*what?*"

"The vampire you wish to kill. You think *I* am him, and I won't fault you for the mistake. It's a common one," Azrael said with a heavy sigh and moved back from me, though his steady gaze never left me.

"What are you talking about?"

The vampire began to vanish into the mist, and I moved forward, wincing as my broken foot hit against a rock beneath the water. I chased after him, snaking my hand out to grab hold of his arm without thinking.

He froze as my hand connected with his warm skin beneath the water, and I remembered where we were.

That beneath the black surface of the water he was naked. And I was damn near close to it with only my thin panties to cover me. I let him go as though burned by his touch, my body reeling from the oppressive weight of his vampiric energy.

Azrael rolled his shoulders back and I noticed for the first time how *ripped* he was. With broad shoulders and arms that looked to be close to the size of my thighs.

Stop it, Rose.

"His name is Raphael. We were born under the same moon."

Was he trying to tell me he had a *twin*?

Yeah. Right. Like I would be believing that. I scoffed. He just wanted me to cooperate. He would say whatever he needed to get what he wanted from me. His kind had no honor.

No code.

Besides his whole theory about my bloodline reeked of bullshit. It was impossible for vampires to walk in sunlight, no matter what this fucking lunatic thought. He had me going with that one. I would do anything to give my guys back that one small thing. To make their new immortal lives that much easier. But I'd had time to think while I'd been all alone in that cell he called a room. And the more I thought about it, the more *insane* it sounded.

What he proposed to do simply wasn't possible. Which left me stuck in this cave belowground with a murdering psychopath who was basically trying to sell me on the theory that he had the cure to vampirism.

If I didn't know any better, I would have to start thinking *I* was the crazy one for believing him at all.

A muscle in his jaw twitched.

"I don't believe you."

"Should I care?

Grinding my teeth to keep my taloned fingers from striking out, I managed to keep myself in check at the barely concealed taunt in his tone. "I want to see them," I spat, unable to keep the venom from my voice as I backed away, keeping a good three feet of space between us. "The guys I was with when you captured me—I want to see they are unharmed before I'll do *anything* to help you."

The vampire exhaled as though exasperated. Bored with my insistent requests.

The smug prick.

"I'll fight," I added, practically hissing. "I'll make it a nightmare for you to do—well, to do *whatever the hell* it is you want me to do."

I thought I saw him flinch at the threat and a glimmer of hope made me even more brazen. "But," I said, annunciating the word. "If you just give me this one reque—"

In the blink of an eye Azrael was right in front of me, his eyes boring into mine. His body beneath the water brushing against my nipples. What I thought was his cock brushed against my navel. But the feel of his flesh on mine wasn't the worst part.

The worst part was the way my heart slammed in my chest. How I couldn't look away as his compulsion took hold of me like a clenched fist around my heart and tendrils of iron around my mind.

I fought him with everything I had, my teeth bared to try to shake the force of his compulsion. I squirmed under his gaze like a rat under a microscope. A whimper escaped my lips and a tremor ran down my spine when I realized I couldn't break free. He was too strong.

It was no use.

"You *will* obey me," he growled, his deep voice bellowing in the cavern. He had a crazed look in his eyes as he pushed the command into me, and I buckled under the weight of it.

No.

Fuck.

No!

"Yes."

"Fuck…*you*," I said between gritted teeth.

Azrael grinned, and some of the malice left his eyes. I felt his hold on me weaken and I managed to break the connection, dropping my head so he couldn't compel me again. "You're stronger than I thought," he said, and I shoved myself away from his touch, feeling utterly violated. My body shaking. "I'll take you to see your *friends*. But then you *will* do as I say."

My lips parted and my stomach dropped.

"Whether you like it or not."

4

Azrael hadn't spoken since our little chat in the devil's spring. He just got out of the bath and gave me a full and unobstructed view of his backside in the flickering torchlight and waited for me to follow him.

Still dripping, we made our way through the underground passageways. He matched my slow, hobbling pace, staying only two steps ahead of me the entire time. But when I began to see light up ahead, I realized he wasn't taking me back to my chamber, or even outside into the fresh air to go to my guys as I'd hoped.

No. The light I saw was too bright to be natural. Too blue-hued and fluorescent. And as we approached the open mouth of the chamber ahead, I gaped in awe at what was contained within. The underground room was enormous, built right into the rock walls of the cave. It was a…a lab?

Stainless steel, hard glass, and microscopes. Bright lights and Bunsen burners. It looked so out of place among the jagged stone and mineral deposits. The floor here was smooth, too. It'd been ground down into a polished surface and if my feel could've sighed, they would have.

After the long trek through the tunnels, even my *not broken* foot was beginning to grow sore.

"Come," Azrael said finally and walked to a long steel table, gesturing to a stool beside it.

Swallowing hard, I lifted my chin—not moving a muscle. "I said I wasn't going to help you until you—"

"*I'm* helping *you*," he hissed, turning his sights on me. His blue eye looked brighter in the white light, and the way it played over his face deepened the shadows under his jaw and cheekbones. It made him look even more menacing. If that were even possible. But it also made his muscled chest and sculpted back look more defined. And his long hair, still damp from the water, seem darker, bringing out the lighter flecks in his eyes and the natural shade of his lips.

I furrowed my brow. "Help me?" I asked, incredulously, eyeing the equipment laid out on the table that, to me, looked distinctly surgical.

"Your foot," he explained, gruffly. "It's broken.

It's maddening watching you hobble around like that."

Total. Dick.

But truth be told, I'd been eager to get the bones set since I awoke. I wouldn't be doing any killing or running until it was healed properly.

"Come," he repeated. "Before I change my mind and leave you a cripple."

Barely able to conceal a scathing retort, I clenched my fists almost to the point of breaking skin, and attempted to stomp over to the stool. I only managed a weak limp-stomp, but I hoped it got the message across. I was pissed. And the only reason I was accepting help from him was because I didn't want to fucking hobble anymore either.

"Sit," he commanded with a glance in my direction. Our eyes met and the force of his compulsion washed me like a wave, shoving me back and down until I was sitting like a good little girl in the stool.

I shook my head and blinked away the compelling force. "Don't fucking do that!" I barked at him. "Don't compel me."

"Then listen."

Goddamned, motherfucking ass—

"Damnit, woman! Would you stop it with your infernal cursing? It's an insult to the ears. Are you not properly educated?"

I blew out a breath to keep from yelling. "I'll make you a deal, since my *infernal cursing* is such an insult to your ears, I'll work on toning it down if you stay the *fuck* out of my head!" I couldn't help how the words ended in a shout. I couldn't help the curse there, either.

I *hated* that he could read my thoughts.

Azrael lifted his eyes to the ceiling and brushed the hair from his face. "Goddess save me," he whispered under his breath. I wasn't even sure I'd heard him right.

He pulled up a stool opposite me and gestured to my leg. "Give me your foot."

Begrudgingly, I lifted my leg and placed it in his lap. The bones on the top of my foot were clearly malformed, making it impossible for me to put my foot flat on the ground. I'd had to limp along using the side of my foot. Whatever damage had been done caused it to pull inward.

It looked super gross.

"Would you like something to bite down on?" Azrael asked as he gingerly took my foot into his hands, feeling along my skin to find the areas he would need to re-set. I seriously hoped he knew what the hell he was doing.

I shook my head. I'd dealt with worse. And the pain always faded pretty—

The sickening *snap* and follow-up grind of bone being moved into place was all but drowned out by my blood-curdling scream as he jammed the bones back into their proper place.

Tears stung my eyes and I inhaled a broken breath as the initial pain dulled into something more manageable.

I resisted the urge to let loose a string of profanities that would have made even *me* blush. My body shook from the searing agony radiating up my leg. Through the haze of watery vision, I watched as Azrael put damp casting material on my foot and up the back of my leg, adding another heavy piece the front. I sucked in a breath as it connected with the still tender flesh. But Azrael never stopped, he worked quickly, his expert fingers wrapping the tensor bandage around the cast to hold it in place.

The instant he finished, I leaned forward and smacked his hands away, drawing my leg down from his lap to place it lightly on the floor. "You could have *warned* me," I seethed.

If he'd given me a 1, 2, 3 count I could have contained myself. I just wasn't ready.

Azrael lifted a brow at me. And was that a smirk on his stupid handsome face? Murderers shouldn't be allowed to be so damned pretty.

"You think I'm pretty?"

"I hate you."

5

It looked like Azrael was going to keep his word.

I'd refused his offer to help me back to my chamber, and when I got there, I was excited to see a new tray of food had been placed on the bed. Azrael rolled his eyes at the busted bedframe, but said '*I'll be back in an hour to fetch you. I'll take you to see them. But then you'll* behave *yourself.*'

Behave? Like I was some kind of fucking animal, when *he* was the one who…I didn't allow myself to finish the thought. The cat was out of the bag now. Azrael knew I wanted him dead. He knew that *I* knew he was the one who killed my mother and almost killed me, too.

I didn't believe what he said about having a twin for even a second.

But even as I thought it, an inkling of doubt

slunk up my spine. I remembered that night clear as a bell. And the man who held me captive in this cave didn't seem like the same man. The man who killed my mother wouldn't have re-set my broken bones, would he?

He wouldn't feed me and make sure I was clean.

And he certainly wouldn't take me to see that my guys were alright—no matter how annoyingly adamant I was about it.

I'd seen the malice in those mis-matched eyes. I'd witnessed the red fury and the maniacal smile.

I didn't want to believe it, but I had to consider the option that this *Azrael* person was telling me the truth.

The fact that I'd actually heard the name Raphael before, from Frost's own mouth no less, gave me hope that seeing my guys were alright would also help me to solve the riddle that was my captor. And if he was lying, then seeing them might give me the opportunity I needed to kill him.

I knelt to the floor and reached beneath the bed, tugging my makeshift stake out of its hiding place. The woman had lain out clothes for me on the bed next to the tray of food, and I was grateful they weren't nearly as skimpy as what I'd had on when I arrived here.

A thick woolen sweater that looked like it came from the reject bin at a thrift store and a pair of jeans two sizes too big. They looked atrocious and smelled like mothballs and dryer lint, but the woolen sweater worked wonders for allowing me to conceal the stake in the waistband of the too-big jeans.

I made the mistake of getting caught without a weapon not so long ago, and I wouldn't make that same mistake again.

Once I was ready, all I had left to do was wait.

The hour passed agonizingly slow and I bounced my good leg on the floor, testing the other one with varying degrees of pressure to see if the cast was ready to be removed. It didn't hurt anymore and that was a good sign. I'd see if Azrael wouldn't mind removing it before we left. I didn't want to show up to see the guys in the thing. They would just worry.

And I couldn't very well stake a fucker as fast as Azrael was if I couldn't lunge properly.

I felt the vampire approaching before I saw him. I gulped and stood, ready to demand he take me to remove the cast before we left. If he refused, I'd just do it myself—likely at the expense of a few fingernails. But the usually perfectly sharp points were already all busted up and broken anyway.

I needed a manicure *bad*. But I didn't think I'd be convincing fuckface to make a pit stop at a salon along the way.

A low whistle had me pinching my brows together and I looked up to see that it wasn't Azrael who was in the doorway, but another vampire. I could feel the otherness with him, but it wasn't even remotely as strong as the aura Azrael possessed.

The vampire leaned against the doorway, his arms crossed over his chest, his jet-black hair falling forward to cover his slim face and small, beady eyes.

Ew.

This guy had pedophile written all over him.

"Where's Azrael?" I asked calmly, taking stock of the vamp. He didn't look to have any weapons on him, but the slim bulge in his left pocket looked a lot like a switchblade. He wore an ill-fitting leather jacket over a lime green t-shirt and jeans that rose low on his hips, exposing a good amount of uncovered hipbones.

The vamp's lips parted, and I watched in disgust as he ran his tongue over his front teeth, his fangs slipping low. "He sent me to fetch you," he said.

Great.

When I didn't make a move forward, the vampire pushed off the wall and eyed me up and down, a taunting sneer curling his lips. "Move," he commanded, leering.

I stepped forward and the vampire moved out of my way. "After you."

I *really* wasn't in the mood for this shit. Why hadn't Azrael just come, himself? Why would he send douchy-mcgee to fetch me? Did he doubt my disdain for his kind?

Just because I couldn't kill him—well, not yet,

anyway—didn't mean there was anything to stop me from killing his hired help.

I only had one stake, though, so I'd play nice unless he gave me a reason not to.

The darkness of the tunnel swallowed us up as we left my cell and I felt along the wall, dragging my heavy foot along behind me. The vampire guided me with curt commands of *left* and *right* as we went.

It was all kinds of boring and I really felt like I was in need of a bit of fun. "I never caught your name?" I called back to the vamp.

"Just keep moving."

"Or what?" I teased with a wicked grin I hoped he couldn't see in the dark.

Just because I didn't want to waste my stake on the fucker, didn't mean I couldn't at least have a little fun riling him up.

"Or I'll fucking tear your throat out," he hissed.

"Oooh," I said in an ominous, spooky tone. "I'm terrified."

I chuckled. "Don't think Azrael would appreciate that."

He took the bait and I readied myself for impact as he grabbed hold of my shoulder and slammed me into the rough stone wall. After the initial shock of the air leaving my lungs, I laughed, a little bit of blood coating my tongue from where I bit the edge of it.

The vampire growled into my face. His hot,

stale breath fanned over my face. I could just make out his silhouette in the shadows. The curve of his jaw and the shine of his hair. The glint of white fangs as they lowered the rest of way.

Oh crap.

Why did I have to bleed?

That wasn't part of the plan. I clamped my mouth shut to try to seal off the scent of it from him.

But who was I kidding? Hadn't I wanted this? Hoped for it.

It'd been far too long since I sent one of these bastards to their true death. And this one wasn't like my guys. He wasn't smart, or kind. He didn't live by a code like they did. I'd spotted the blood stain on his t-shirt and the blush in his cheeks from the moment he walked into my room.

If his predatory smile wasn't enough, he was literally *wearing* the remains of his last meal. Did vampires not know what the hell a napkin was? *Christ*, the number of times I'd caught them with human blood on their clothes was astounding.

I didn't go around with ketchup and blue-slushie all over myself, did I? No. Because I wasn't a three-year-old.

The vampire slipped his leg between mine and I choked on a sound of disgust as he tried to press himself up against me.

He leaned in to bite me, and I kneed him *hard* in

the groin. He bent low, gasping for breath. Not even vampires were immune to a good knock to the family jewels. While he was down, I pulled him head-first into the stone wall, moving out of the way as I did. His head *cracked* against the stone and I heard him let loose a sad, low mewling sound.

He'd be back up real fast if I didn't hurry. Hobbling around in the stupid cast wasn't making this any easier, either. I jammed my hand into his pocket and drew out the…pocket vagina? It was hard to see in the dark, but as I twirled it between my fingers, I saw the *lips* on the business end of it and gagged.

Seriously?

Disgusted, I dropped the thing as though it were diseased—*and honestly, it probably was*—and regained my composure just in time to see him regaining his.

Oh shit…

His back was still to me as his hunched position began to right itself. I was about to draw my stake, ready to sacrifice all the hard work I'd put in making it to waste it on this *lowlife* leech when the heavy feeling of Azrael's presence rushed me like a red flag before a bull.

I had just enough time to move myself back before he was upon us.

Or more accurately, upon the vampire who I'd taunted into attacking me.

Their movements were a blur and all I heard

was the scuffle, over in less than two seconds with a crunch, a sucking sound, and a nasty gurgle. Then the winner rose, and the loser's lifeless body slumped against the hard rock.

Azrael came to stand in front of me. I could tell it was him from the broad shoulders and the tickle of his hair against my cheek as he leaned down to inspect me. "Are you—"

"Well that was rude," I told him, flipping my hair back as I stepped past him. "I wasn't done playing with him, yet."

He growled before shoving me against the wall with his forearm pressed against my upper chest. It made it hard to breathe, but I knew he was going easy. He could've crushed me if he wanted to, but he didn't.

I stared him down and he stared back, the fury rippled off him in waves. His face was twisted in a snarl that would have made any man tremble.

I had the sense to thank my lucky stars that I seemed to have something he wanted. Without that, I'd be long dead by now.

All at once, Azrael's expression changed, and his forearm disappeared from my chest. I fell the half a foot back to the ground, almost falling over from the awkwardness of my cast. I caught my breath and moved my hand to squeeze a sudden stitch in my side.

"You probably did me a favor." Azrael nudged

the body out of the pathway with his foot and I flinched as I felt his hand come around my arm, but relaxed when I realized he was just helping me not to trip over the corpse as he pulled me after him. “I never liked that one, anyway.”

Okay…

Not what I was expecting.

“Yeah,” I said sarcastically, tugging my arm out of his grasp to follow behind him. “You’re welcome.”

6

"You have got to be kidding me."

Azrael led me into a wide section of the cave. If I knew he was leading us someplace close to the exit, I would have been paying a lot more attention to the route we were taking. As it was, I could barely remember the last two turns we took to get here, still miffed that he'd stolen my kill. Behind us was the tunnel we'd emerged from, and several others like it, but ahead was a much wider opening, and if I wasn't mistaken, it looked to be brighter than all the others.

"Not kidding," he responded, moving away from me to speak to a man wearing a pristine suit jacket standing next to a hearse.

Yeah, *a hearse.*

But that wasn't the best part.

Outside of the hearse, on a raised platform, was a coffin.

A fucking coffin.

I stalked over to the thing and looking inside, clenching my teeth. It was clearly meant for one person, but it was bigger than your average burial box. Inside the polished mahogany exterior was cushioned and covered in black silk. A satin pillow rested at the head of it.

"Azrael," I ground out. "I am *not* climbing in this coffin with you."

Azrael turned from his conversation with the man in the suit, the glimmer of challenge in his eyes. Then he turned back to the compelled hearse driver and said, "It seems your services are no longer required, my friend. The lady doesn't wish to see her companions, anymore."

My breath caught. "Wait!" I practically shouted as the driver made to turn. Azrael stopped him from getting back into the vehicle. My breathing had picked up and I glanced from the coffin to Azrael and back again, my heart thrumming in my ears. My stomach was ready to heave.

I *hated* small spaces. It was why I didn't like elevators. It was why, in this godforsaken cave, I felt like I could only breath halfway. Like there was a weight on my chest at all times.

If I thought the air here was stale, I cringed to imagine what it would be like stuck in a coffin with an immortal undead guy for…how long had he said? *Six hours.*

I steeled myself, dragging in an unsteady breath. "Fine," I said through gritted teeth. "I'll do it."

Azrael clapped his hands together and grinned at me. "Excellent."

He nodded to the driver who resumed his stoic stance with his hands behind his back, waiting for us to get inside the coffin so he could roll us into the back of the hearse and drive us where we needed to go.

My pulse wouldn't calm as Azrael made his way back over to me, but I tried my best to appear calm. "Tell me again, why exactly do we need to get in a fucking coffin?"

Azrael frowned at my cursing, but right now I didn't care about our little bargain. This was going to be *hell.*

"It will take us six hours to arrive in Baton Rouge," he said, and I ignored the fact that he seemed to know without my having to tell him where they lived. Had he always known? I shivered. He wasn't bluffing when he said he would hurt the people I cared about if I didn't cooperate, was he? "It's about midday now. But leaving at this hour will allow us to arrive after sunset. Then we'll have time for your little *visit*…and have time to get back on the road before sunrise."

"So, it's to protect *you* from the sunlight." I stated.

"Yes," he said, unapologetically. "And I can't trust you anywhere out of my line of sight it appears. Compulsion or not."

He wasn't wrong. I was the fucking *queen* of loopholes.

Then I thought of something. "Wait. Didn't you say that *my blood* was like some sort of cosmic sunscreen? Can't you just use some so that we don't have to," I glared down at the box of doom. "You know—shack up in a death box?"

He chuckled, and shockingly, I found the sound to be kind of pleasant. I shook my head to clear it and tried to replace the traitorous feeling with the right one: disgust. Shame made heat rise to my cheeks and I dug my jagged nails into my palms to rid myself of it.

"Are you offering?" he asked dangerously, stepping in with a lusty gleam in his eyes and a twist to his lush lips. His hulking frame blocked what little light there was, and I cursed myself at the shudder that ran through me at the prospect of his ancient teeth piercing my flesh.

I shoved him away, and his eyes widened in surprise. "*Hell* no."

Azrael shrugged, suddenly the picture of emotionless calm. "I wouldn't take it from you, Rose," he told me, turning to jump up onto the table and step into the coffin. "I certainly won't be the first one to test the theory. Synthesizing your blood into a combatant against sunlight is going to take time." He set his eyes on me with a cutting look. "A *lot* of time."

Of course, he wouldn't be the first to try it. The great and terrible Azrael wouldn't deign to put *himself* in danger. Oh no. He'd rather watch one of his lackeys burn to a crisp.

And now he was telling me I was stuck here for a *lot of time*. How long was a *lot of time*, exactly?

Fuck my life.

"Coming?" Azrael asked after a moment's hesitation on my part.

I tried to climb onto the raised table thing to get into the coffin, but my cast was difficult to maneuver. I bent to try to pry it off, but I could barely get my fingers inside the top of it to get any sort of leverage.

In a flash, Azrael was out of the coffin, off the table, and knelt in front of me.

I recoiled, but he already had his hands on my cast, one on either side. He had the thing broken off in two perfect halves within the blink of an eye.

I tried not to look impressed.

He took hold of my bare foot, inspecting it, feeling around the areas where the bones had been broken. "A perfect setting," he muttered to himself, as though giving himself a pat on the back.

I groaned, tugging my foot out of his hands, and jumped up onto the platform, my body going rigid as I forced myself into the box.

Sitting in the middle of it, I curled my arms around my knees, trying to soothe the riotous beating of my heart.

Azrael, calm as you please, stepped into the box with me, nudging me as he laid down flat on his back. That feeling of *otherness* was sending shivers skittering over the surface of my skin, leaving goose-flesh in their wake.

The driver approached us, drawing the lid from the back of the hearse. It had shining silver knobs on it spaced at intervals down the length. With a jolt, I looked down at the rim of the coffin and found where the latches would catch, effectively *locking* us inside.

"Can't have you trying to tear the lid off mid-trip, now can I?"

The worst part of that was—I hadn't even thought of doing that. Why wasn't I searching for any and every option available to me to kill him?

Azrael nudged me with the tips of his fingers, and I peered back to see a smug look on his stupid handsome face. "You'll need to lay down, Rose," he said, his voice rich with sarcasm.

There was barely more than half a foot of available space next to the massive, hulking form of Azrael. I had no idea how I was supposed to fit.

Either reading my mind, or perhaps seeing me frown at the smidgen of free space, Azrael scooched a bit more to the side and then quirked a brow at me as though to say *this alright for you, princess?*

Fucker.

Wholly unable to conceal the slight tremble now, I closed my eyes and laid back, having to wiggle around a bit to find a spot that would allow me to lay flat enough so as not to impede the lid being put on.

I squeezed my eyes tightly shut as Azrael lifted an arm to put around me, it was the only way I was going to be able to lay flat against the bottom.

It's not him, I told myself. *It's Frost.*

It's Frost who's holding you.

And you're not in a coffin.

You're snuggling in a warm bed.

It's fine.

Everything is—

The lid fell into place with an ominous thud, and what little light there was behind my eyelids vanished into a deep and total blackness.

Each *click* of the latches being turned into locking position made me flinch.

The scent of him coiled around me like a fog and I hated that he smelled good. Woodsy, like white birch, with an undertone of something sweet, yet earthy—like African violets and rain.

"I'm going to murder you," I whispered to

Azrael in the dark through clenched teeth, my fingers clawing into the material of his shirt.

Azrael's laughter echoed in the box as the driver rolled us into the back of the hearse and started the engine.

The unfeeling prick could laugh all he wanted. One day I would make good on that promise.

7

I was right.

The six-hour drive was torture.

We were only about an hour into it when my self-assurances began to slip. It helped to focus on the roar of the engine, and the tires chewing pavement below us, but that only worked to a point. Every so often—and by *so often* I mean about every two minutes—I would remember that we were in a fucking coffin in the back of a fucking hearse and that I was basically *cuddling* with the man who I thought murdered my mother.

The *vampire*, I corrected my thoughts, who almost killed my guys and kidnapped me.

I maneuvered my body to try to put some space between us, turning so I was facing him instead of being awkwardly half on my side and half on my back. But to my dismay, he readjusted himself, too, pressing himself against my front.

Coffin hog.

"Is that a stake or are you just happy to be here?"

The joke took me so much by surprise that I just stared into the dark in stunned silence and horror.

It made jokes?

Azrael had his hand halfway down my pants before I could do anything to stop him. I gasped as he withdrew the long piece of whittled bedpost. I tried to snatch it back, but no matter how hard I tried to pry it out of his fingers, it remained there, as though encased in cement instead of flesh.

"Give it back," I hissed.

"As you wish," he said, and tossed it back to me, but since I couldn't see anything in the all-consuming dark, it hit against my temple and I groaned, placing it firmly between my legs since I had no better place for it.

I couldn't believe the cocky fucker actually gave it back.

Didn't he know what I planned to do with it?

"If it were that easy to kill me, I'd be long dead by now."

We went over a pothole and my stomach dropped; my mind thrown back into claustrophobic panic mode. My chest grew tight and my breaths came short and fast—heart pounding anew. Sweat beaded on my brow.

"Tell me," I said, willing to try *anything* to distract myself. I was starting to feel disoriented and the last thing I wanted was to pass out in this coffin with Azrael. I needed to keep my head. "How old are you, exactly?"

I heard him make a popping sound with his lips, as though considering whether or not he should tell me. After a few more moments of paralyzing dread as the walls of the box felt like they were closing in, he answered. "Over a millennia. I can't pinpoint the exact number of years."

"What?"

I must've heard him wrong. There was no way he could possibly be—

"I was born on the immortal continent of Emeris."

No. Fucking. Way.

There were two immortal continents shrouded from the mortal eye. A human hadn't ever set foot on either of them. They weren't on our maps. No sailor had ever even so much as *seen* them on the horizon.

The magic that kept them separate from our mortal lands also worked as a sort of human repellant. From what I knew, any ships that managed to get even remotely close had sunk in some form of storm.

I always thought they were somewhere near Bermuda. Within that triangle everyone was so wary of.

But I would never know.

I didn't know much of anything about them other than that they existed. Courtesy of a very chatty vamp who I'd gleaned information from before I'd staked him. It wasn't the sort of information I was looking for, but I'd allowed him to finish, finding the new bit of info quite interesting.

I always thought the blood sucker was lying, but after hearing Ethan speak about the place, and now Azrael, too, I had to believe it was real.

"And why did you come here? Why not stay where you belong? Terrorize your own people? Hmm?"

His body stiffened next to mine. "I didn't have a choice," he practically growled. "None of us did."

What the hell did that mean?

"Your puny mortal mind couldn't comprehend it."

"Fuck you."

He snorted.

As the distraction faded and the panic began to rise again, a small whimper left my lips and my chest felt so tight I thought it would implode.

I needed to get out of here.

Azrael groaned.

The vampire moved himself so he was on his

side, too, facing me. I kept my eyes firmly closed even though if I'd opened them, I wouldn't have been able to see anyway.

"Rose?" he said gruffly.

I just focused on breathing.

"Rose, open your eyes."

How could he see in here? It was so dark.

"No," I breathed. "It makes it worse."

"I'll make it better."

Confused, I opened my eyes for a split second and felt an iron vise curl itself around my heart and mind. *Shit.*

"Sleep," Azrael commanded, and I felt my body sag. All my bunched, aching muscles turned to jelly, and my bones unlocked. My head lolled back, and my eyelids fluttered closed.

I drifted into a deep and dreamless sleep.

8

I couldn't be sure what woke me, but as I blinked back into the present, I found myself surrounded in darkness.

There was a cushioned wall to my back, a warm body pressing in against me and an unyielding surface both beneath and above me.

Where the hell am I?

My heart began to race and vaguely, I thought I heard someone say to *calm down,* but I was already clawing at the surface of the box I was trapped inside, breathing fast, breaking nails. I tried to turn to put myself in a position to kick at the wood, but I couldn't raise my leg high enough to do it, I didn't have enough space.

A small, broken sound came out of my mouth before I could stifle it and then I felt movement. The box was being moved.

I shouted, and as I heard little *clink, clink* sounds, I worried that something was about to explode.

"*Rose*," A voice shouted and in a moment of clarity, I recognized the deep, rich, baritone. It was…Azrael. I was in a coffin with…Azrael.

We were in a cave, but we were going to—

Where had we been going?

It all came back in a rush and I lashed out, punching Azrael as hard as I could without the ability to reel back. "*You asshole.* I told you not to compel me!"

"You were having a panic attack," he said calmly, as though he didn't even feel the hit.

The groan I let escape sounded more like a growl.

"Your welcome," he added as the lid above us loosened and then lifted.

I was up and scrambling out of the evil box in a heartbeat. My lungs protested at the amount of fresh, unrestricted air that I was pulling in greedily through my nostrils and open mouth. I coughed and my head cleared. As the dizziness passed, I reached down and grabbed my makeshift stake from the pavement where it fell in my haste to escape and tucked it back into my lose-fitting jeans.

As I righted myself, I blinked to clear my vision and waited for my eyes to adjust to the light.

We were parked at the side of a two-way street. A lot at our backs and across the street, a line of shops, all closed for the night. By the position of the moon, it had to be around ten at night. Maybe a bit later than that.

My eyes narrowed on the enormous corner building down the way. It was old, colonial style, with fancy trim and edging—half-columns spaced evenly between wide panes of glass on the bottom level. The top level had the same, except there, every window was blacked out.

But it wasn't the building that caught my eye—it was the decal on the window facing us. It was a pair of crescent moons back to back with old fashioned script like writing beneath that read *Moonlit Ink.*

Below that was a sign posted on the inside that read *Opens at midnight. Closes when I say so.*

Squinting more closely, I saw that they had two roses worked into the logo design. That couldn't have been an accident.

I smirked.

My heart swelled and I resisted the urge to immediately beeline for the building.

Swallowing, I made my voice as steady as I could. "Are they up there?"

I considered the blacked-out windows and wondered if they could see outside.

Azrael stepped up next to me and nodded. "Yes."

I didn't ask how he knew. Maybe he could sense

them. Or maybe the fucker had x-ray vision, who knew…it didn't matter, anyway.

Azrael had kept his word. And he hadn't lied about them being unharmed. Though I wouldn't fully believe it until I saw it for myself.

I moved to cross the quiet street, but Azrael stopped me with a brusque sound in his throat. "Remember our bargain," he said. "You see, they're alright and then you come back with me. You do as I ask. Or else…" he trailed off.

He didn't need to say it again. How could I forget?

Either I did as he asked, or he would hurt the people I loved.

I glanced back at the tall building on the corner and my bottom lip quivered.

Damn.

Ignoring the inner voice that was screaming at me, I removed the stake from my jeans and tossed it to Azrael, who caught it easily midair and grinned. "Good choice," he crooned. "Now let's go meet the family, shall we?"

The door to go up to the second-floor apartment was plain black, nondescript. It didn't even have a handle on it.

A panel with a speaker box and a single off-white button rested on the wall to the right. Azrael and I stepped off the street and onto the stoop and I gulped. "Do you *have* to come with me?"

"Afraid so."

I pursed my lips, my finger hovering a mere inch from pressing the button on the receiver. "And if they try to kill you?"

It was a distinct possibility. He kidnapped me and almost killed them. If they recognized him—they'd be going for the throat. And I didn't think Azrael would take too kindly to an attack from three rather large vampires—no matter how young they were in comparison.

All thoughts of ganging up on him with my guys had vanished the moment I'd seen the tattoo shop—those roses in the logo. If we tried to fight him, I had no doubt at least one of us would fall. If not more than one.

If not *all*.

Now that I knew he was over a thousand years old, I was reconsidering my position. I'd have to relegate myself to the disappointing fact that I was stuck with him until he decided otherwise.

Azrael fixed me with a look that said he wasn't even remotely worried about it. "Don't worry so much. I won't hurt them. Not so long as you keep your end of the bargain."

I jabbed the buzzer before I could change my mind.

A gruff and smoky voice shouted over the intercom, "What?"

"Blake?"

The line went dead. There was a thudding sound from inside the building, the quick steps down the stairs like the beating of a drum.

The door was wrenched open and he was standing there, his hair disheveled and mouth agape. He was wearing a simple white undershirt and black jeans. His dark hair glistening as though he'd just come out of a shower.

"Rose?" he asked as though he wasn't sure, his voice not the steady, detached one I'd heard just days ago. Now, it was slightly strangled.

"Hey handsome."

His gaze flicked to the vampire standing at my back and his expression changed. His eyes darkened and his fangs slid low to puncture his bottom lip. He growled and I watched all the muscles in his arms and shoulders flex, poised for the kill.

"Blake!" I shouted to get his attention. It worked. He glanced at me for a fraction of a second and I was able to shake my head. "Don't."

Just then the thunderous sound of double footfalls thudded down into the entry. Frost muscled his way into place beside Blake and Ethan shoved them both out of the way as he hit the bottom step.

"You're alive," Frost breathed, frozen in shock.

Ethan pulled me into his arms and held me so tight it was almost painful. I felt his chest tighten. He wasn't breathing. "Ethan," I breathed into the crook of his neck. "I'm alright."

"*Rafe*," Frost seethed, and I turned to find both Blake and Frost in fighting stances, their fangs protruding, and hand curled into white-knuckled fists.

Rafe?

So, I had been right, then? He was lying to me the whole time?

I cursed the sting of betrayal I felt. You couldn't feel betrayed unless there was trust to begin with. I'd never trusted him. Had I?

Azrael—*er*—Rafe, or whoever he was cocked his head at them. "You know my brother?"

Frost's brows lowered, and Blake's jaw twitched.

I thanked my lucky starts they weren't stupid enough to go full bore and attack him. As Ethan positioned me slightly behind him, we backed away so I was surrounded by the warm bodies of my guys. Ethan never released me but kept me tucked into his side with an arm tightly wrapped around my shoulder. Frost reached back to squeeze my hand. I held tight to it.

If only they knew that they couldn't shield me this time.

They couldn't save me at all.

But it was sweet of them to try.

"Your brother?" Ethan asked, his tone clipped.

Frost stomped out onto the stoop and my heart jumped into my throat. "Frost! Don't—"

The hulking brute stopped a few inches from the

ancient vampire, and I was surprised to see they were the same height. Frost outweighed Azrael by at least fifty pounds, but what Azrael lacked in size, he made up for in malice. He stared down Frost as though he were a bug to be quashed.

"If you hurt him, I'll *never* cooperate. I'll fight tooth and—"

"Yes. Yes. *I know*," Azrael said, waving me off, annoyed.

Frost seemed to be studying Azrael, seething and red-faced as he did, but Frost was no idiot. He didn't move to strike.

"Azrael?" Frost breathed the name as a question after a moment and I saw the muscles in his shoulders droop, but only a fraction.

"*There* you go. For someone who knows my dear brother, it's quite easy to tell the difference, is it not?"

Frost staggered back, shaking his head.

I noticed Blake wasn't coiled to strike anymore, either. His fangs were still out, and I had to admit that they somehow suited him, and his fists were still clenched, but he didn't look like he was about to tear someone's throat out anymore.

"Are you sure?" Ethan's voice was strained as he asked Frost, his grip on me loosening slightly.

"I'm sure," Frost replied, stepping further back from the vamp. "It's not Rafe."

So…wait…

They *knew* the vampire who killed my mother this entire time?

I stepped out of Ethan's arms. "Did you know that Raphael was the vampire who killed my mother?" I asked them, trying not to feel utterly betrayed. Why would they keep that from me?

Frost turned to face me; his face hard as he ran a wide hand through his white-blond hair. "Yes," he said in a breath. "At least, we believed he was. We've been tracking him for a long time."

"And he's been tracking *you*," Blake added, his voice dripping venom. "He's the one who put the bounty on your head, Rose."

I struggled to keep up with what they were telling me. To connect the dots. "That's not right," I told them all. "It couldn't have been this *Raphael* vamp. He's over a thousand years old—there's *no way* my mother could have compelled him."

It just wasn't possible.

I felt the power of Azrael's compulsion. I never felt anything like it. I knew beyond a shadow of doubt that I wouldn't *ever* be able to hold him under the power of my own inferior compulsion. I knew that I would *never* be able to deny him.

"Impressive, isn't it?" Azrael mused, his eyes alight with an emotion close to excitement. "If I'd know the woman had a surviving heir, I'd have been searching for you *much* sooner."

My head was suddenly pounding as I struggled

to make everything they were saying fit within the confines of my mind.

"She couldn't have..." I trailed off.

Azrael fixed me with a knowing stare. "Oh, but it is, my dear Rose," he said. "The compulsion of an untainted Vocari would prove stronger than some of the eldest vampires I know. But the compulsion of a *female* untainted Vocari would rival even my own... with years of practice, anyway."

I was flabbergasted. The fuck? So, he was saying that if I practiced enough—if I trailed my ability hard enough—that I could compel him?

The guys seemed just as confused as I was, and I could already see the gears and cogs turning in Ethan's mind.

When no one spoke, all of us mulling over this new tidbit of information, Azrael held out a hand for me and my stomach dropped. "Come, Rose. You've seen they're unharmed, as promised. Time to go."

Ethan shoved me behind them into the stairwell as they formed a wall of muscle at my front, blocking Azrael from me.

Idiots.

I shoved between Frost and Blake, trying to pass, my chest tight.

"You aren't going anywhere, Rosie," Frost growled. "Just stay behind us."

I groaned. "We had a deal," I told them. "My

cooperation in exchange for your safety."

"Your cooperation?" Ethan asked, brow furrowed as he glanced at me over his shoulder.

"*Our* safety?" Blake scoffed. "You don't have to worry about us, luv."

Yup. Idiots.

Didn't they know how old Azrael was?

Or were they just that cocky?

"I don't have time for this," Azrael said, pinching the bridge of his nose. "Rose will come with me, and once I'm finished with her, I will happily return her to you, though I don't expect she'll live long without my protection."

Frost's face pinched. He didn't like what Azrael was insinuating; that they weren't enough to protect me. "Where are you taking her?"

I finally manage to get past Frost, though his big hand circled my wrist, stopping me from crossing the five feet of distance between us. I stopped and set a gentle, calming hand on Frost's forearm. "It's alright big guy," I told him. "Once fuckface over there realizes my blood can't do what he thinks it can, he'll let me go." I tried to keep my tone light, but the truth was, I didn't know if he would ever let me leave. Especially if my blood didn't prove to be the missing ingredient he needed.

But they didn't need to know that.

"What is it you want with her blood?" Ethan asked, his tone calmly dangerous. He was grinding his teeth in that way he did when he was keeping from saying what he really wanted to say.

Azrael sighed. "You might as well know," he replied. "For it's the same reason my brother wants to spill it. Rose is the last surviving untainted Vocari—"

"You said that, already," Blake snapped.

Azrael, unperturbed by the injection, continued. "I believe her blood could be the key to lifting the curse," he said plainly. "Or, at least, it could allow for the ability to walk in sunlight."

Ethan paled.

Frost's jaw clenched.

Blake looked like he was thinking up ways to dissect Azrael into tiny pieces and scatter them across the globe.

"That isn't possible." Ethan began grinding his teeth again.

"Isn't it?" Azrael challenged.

Ethan's gaze grew distant as he considered what Azrael said, and then, seemingly deciding something, he snapped his head up. "Take me with you."

It wasn't a question. Not a request at all. Ethan was submitting a demand and by the steely look in his gaze, I knew he would find some way to follow if that demand wasn't met.

Fuck he was hot when he took charge like that. I had a vivid image of him, naked and sweaty between the sheets, taking charge of—

"Rose," Azrael warned. "Do you mind?"

I groaned. "If you don't like what you find in there, stay the fuck out!"

The guys looked between Azrael and I, brows quirked.

"He can read minds," I explained. "Sorry, probably should've mentioned that before."

The guys didn't seem at all surprised to hear it. Frost inhaled sharply and I saw him painstakingly trying to stop his fists from clenching. He didn't like that this other vampire held any sort of sway over me. I could see it in the darkness of his gaze and rigidness of his spine.

He wanted to kill Azrael.

But he knew that no matter how strong he was—he would be no match for the millennia old vamp who was holding me captive.

"Why allow her to come at all if you were just going to drag her away the moment she arrived?" Frost spat, a snarl curling his top lip over his fangs.

Azrael fixed me with a cutting glare. "Because she's stubborn as a mule and annoying as a Strix in heat. She wouldn't shut up about seeing you."

Strix?

"*Sounds about right,*" Blake whispered under his breath and I punched him in the arm.

"Why didn't you just compel her?" Ethan asked, suspicion in the narrowing of his gaze.

A look of disgust crossed Azrael's face. "This

may come as a shock to you, especially if you're familiar with my dear brother's beliefs, but I do not relish what we have become. And I do not *enjoy* bending another's will to my own."

I wasn't buying it. But whatever the true reason was, I was just grateful I'd gotten a chance to see my guys again before I resigned myself to an indeterminate amount of time in a dank fucking cave with a thousand-year-old monster.

A group of young men, drunk by the look of it, were making their way down the street, but as one caught sight of us, he dragged the others to the opposite side of the road. Smart fuckers. Even normal humans could sense the presence of a predator if they were near enough to one.

"Why don't we take this conversation inside?" Frost asked, tilting his head toward the stairwell behind us.

"This conversation is over," Azrael replied, his tone lethal, warning my guys not to argue with him.

I strode forward, shaking off Frost's grip, until I was eye to eye with Azrael. It took me a moment to choke down my pride before I was able to grind out the words, my fists white-knuckled balls at my sides. "Please."

Azrael looked down at me with surprise, considering the simple word. I thought I saw his eyes soften for an instant before his hard mask was back in place. He inhaled sharply, but I spoke again quickly, interrupting him before he could begin. "Let me stay."

Fire flashed in his eyes.

"Let me stay, just for a little while. A week? Hell, I'll take a day! I'll do whatever you want if you just give me some—"

"You have three hours," Azrael said in a deadpan voice. "We leave before dawn."

I couldn't help the elation bubbling up through my core, bringing a smile to my lips. It wasn't much, but it was *something.* I knew he didn't have to offer me this. He could have subdued all three of the guys and dragged me back with him.

He was trying to keep me pliant. Probably hopeful for a patient and willing test subject he wouldn't have to exert energy to compel every five minutes.

"If you don't return with me of your own volition…" Azrael warned, his eyes boring into my soul. I shuddered at the force of his stare, feeling the beginnings of his compulsion taking told. I stifled a whimper, not wanting the guys to attack.

Once his grip lessened, I let out an unrestricted breath and nodded. "I understand."

And then Azrael was gone. My hair whipped around my face at his insane speed and not even my inhuman vision could catch his movements as he vanished into the dark.

9

The guys spirited me up the stairs and into the apartment above the tattoo shop.

We were inside with the door shut behind us before I could get a word in. "Why is he listening to you?" Blake demanded the moment we were sealed inside.

"What's going on, Rose?" Ethan added, worry in the furrow of his brow and the crease in his forehead.

Hot frustration welled up inside me at their inquisition. How the hell was I supposed to know what the fuck was going on? It wasn't like *I* could read Azrael's mind. "I don't know, okay!" I hissed, pushing off the door to stalk past them, deeper into the wide-open space.

It was the truth. I didn't understand why Azrael was giving me these things that I requested instead of just forcing me to do as he pleased. I didn't know why he didn't just kill Blake, Frost, and Ethan. I didn't know what his plans were other than to use my blood as some kind of fucking vampire sunblock. I didn't know *jack shit* other than the fact that if I didn't submit to his demands, he would hurt them.

"I can think of no logical reason why he'd take the risk of bringing you here," Ethan said in a tight voice that told me he *really* didn't like not knowing the reason.

That made two of us.

"Yeah, because everything else he does is *so damned logical?*" I hissed. "The bastard thinks my blood is the cure to vampirism, Ethan. *Sane* and *logical* are not words I would use to describe this creep."

"Actually, it's a valid theory," Ethan retorted, catching scathing looks of incredulity from the other three of us.

Frost's face soured. "You've got to be shitting me."

Ethan shook his head.

Blake ran a hand over his dark hair, his near-black gray eyes flashing in the overhead lights. "Man, don't even say that shit if you aren't serious."

"I am," Ethan said. "It makes sense. I'm not saying he'll succeed. I definitely wouldn't be the first to test his theory. But…Azrael might be on to something."

Now look who drank the kool-aid…

"You had my blood," I said to Frost. "Did you magically gain the ability to walk in sunlight?"

Frost didn't hesitate. "No," he answered. "But it's not like I tried to."

Ugh. I rolled my eyes.

"Is this really how we want to spend our three hours? Arguing about something none of us know is *actually* possible? About the inner workings of a mind that's over a thousand fucking years old?" I asked the guys, changing the subject before I could get good and riled up about the ridiculousness of the whole ordeal.

The three of them shut up, looking me over as though just seeing me for the first time.

"No," Blake growled.

"I doubt it would help," Ethan agreed.

"You aren't going back with him, Rosie," Frost's voice rose above all the others.

I walked back over to him and poked him hard in his big burly chest, I glared up at him. "Oh yes I am, big guy," I near shouted before I could get control of myself. Once I was able, I laid my palms more gently on his heaving chest and sighed. With a cheeky grin I was sure wouldn't reach my eyes, I added, "I'll knock you on your ass myself if you try to attack Azrael. It'll hurt a lot less than whatever he would do to you."

Fury sparked in Frost's gaze.

"Don't make me do it," I warned him, wagging a pointed finger.

If I was being honest, I wasn't entirely sure if I could take Frost. If I got the jump on him, sure. But if he saw it coming, we might be on equal ground. If I compelled him, though…he wouldn't stand a chance, and he knew it.

My compulsion was stronger than his. And I didn't have to test that theory to know it was true.

"Rosie," Frost started, his voice strained.

"It's alright," I told him. "If he was going to kill me, he'd have done it already. He wants to keep me safe probably as much as you do."

Frost wasn't buying that, but some of the tension leaked out of his stiff shoulders and flexed core.

After a few beats of heavy silence, I shook off the unease and decided to make the most of this little visit. Might as well soak it all up while I can. I would need some good memories to get me through the days ahead to be spent in the cold dark.

"So, this is home?" I asked them as I spun on the spot, taking in the space.

Ethan moved to stand beside me. "The closest thing to it we've got."

The interior of the heritage building was just as beautiful and lavish as the exterior. But in here, it'd been updated to suit the modern era. The door we came through opened up into a large central space with a sleek stainless-steel kitchen far to my left, and the bank of covered windows I'd seen from outside lining the wall to my right. In the middle was a sunken living space with cozy looking couches and low coffee tables. A column ran up through the middle of it with an electric fireplace set into it and a large flat screen mounted above.

A glass desk was pushed against the far wall in a little nook. And between there and the kitchen was a wide hallway that I assumed would lead back to where the bathrooms and bedrooms were.

It was huge and it *screamed* my guys. Their clashing and similar tastes reflected in the décor and color scheme. The kitchen was clearly Blake's doing. The clean lines and polished surfaces were so *him*. The desk in the corner, looking like something you might find on a fucking spaceship, was clearly Ethan's.

And the roaring fire and haphazard arrangement of the thick rugs and cozy couches was *definitely* Frost. Underneath all that rage and muscle was an enormous teddy bear who liked soft things and naps. I wondered if he still took naps now that he was immortal. Vampires didn't need to sleep nearly as much as humans did. It was yet another reason to add to the list of reasons why it would be selfish of me not to allow Azrael to at least test his insane theory.

If I could give my guys back even a modicum of normalcy, I had to try.

"Want a tour?" Ethan asked, his muscles still tense and voice still strained.

None of them looked like they would be able to relax while knowing I would have to be removed from their care in only a few short hours.

I sighed heavily.

"What is it?" Ethan asked.

I grinned up at him sheepishly. "Oh nothing," I said in a light tone. "I was just hoping my guys would sack up and show me a good time before I had to leave, but it seems like you're all too distracted."

I pouted, biting on my lower lip.

Come on, I thought. *Take the bait.*

I could use a good distraction. And I could think of no one better to give me one than the three incredibly sexy and dangerous men standing before me.

Blake's jaw twitched, and his eyes glazed over with instant lust.

Frost betrayed no emotion whatsoever, but I didn't miss the unmistakable twitch of his big cock beneath his jeans.

Ethan's ears turned pink at the suggestion, but he lifted his chin and held out his hand to me. I put mine in his. "What my queen wants, my queen gets," he said, and I watched his adams apple bob in his throat as he tugged me in the direction of the darkened hallway.

My stomach fluttered and I shivered as the sensation worked its way out to my extremities, rousing the slumbering dragon in my belly until heat pooled between my thighs. With a bite to my lower lip the little minx in my mind sat up and took notice, too, until I was concocting all sorts of Rose sandwich ideas.

"Aren't you coming?" I called back to the guys, blushing like a maniac. Blake and Frost had taken me together before, so, why did I feel embarrassed for wanting all three of them?

A puzzle of four souls, my mind whispered. That's what we were, weren't we? It just felt…*right.* And this sort of *arrangement* was already widely accepted by vampire kind. Why should it be any different just because I'm human—*er*—*Vocari*.

"Someone should keep watch," Frost grunted, crossing his arms. I could tell he was still pissed off and trying hard to contain himself. He needed to unwind, or he was going to blow his top. And it was never pretty when Frost went full beast mode. He explained those times as black marks in his memory. He didn't see red. He saw *black* and often had little to no memory of what he'd done.

With Azrael prowling outside, I couldn't risk

him losing it without me there to at least attempt to rein him in. "No," I said sweetly, almost teasing, trying my best to keep my tone light so he wouldn't suspect my intentions. "I need some Frost to temper my fire."

A rumbling sound came from his chest as he fixed his stony gaze on me. His shock of white hair shone with strands of silver under the bright lighting. He looked like an angel, and I could almost believe he was one if it weren't for the fangs slipping out from his gums and the lethal gleam in his bright green eyes.

"Somebody needs to—" Frost began again, but Blake was quick to interrupt him, tossing me a quick glance and a miniscule nod that told me he knew *exactly* what I was up to. He knew as well as I did that it would be unwise to leave Frost alone to stew.

"I'll stay," Blake said. "You go on, brother."

Frost's gaze cut to Blake with a note of suspicion, but Blake was already moving to the kitchen, his back to us as he reached into the fridge for a blood bag and then drew a phonebook out of a drawer next to it. My eyes widened for a moment at their store of blood. The fridge had to contain at least fifty bags all stacked neatly on the shelves.

For a moment, my old self cringed in disgust until I remembered they only stole blood because they refused to drink from humans. They didn't want to hurt anyone. This was them being responsible. *Sort of.*

Ethan tugged my hand again and I turned to him with a shy grin. I'd been eager to get him undressed since the moment I saw him in that condo in Atlanta. But he'd been closed off then and still upset that I could never be their vampire bride.

He didn't seem upset anymore, or at least not about that. The tension was still there in his gaze though, no matter how hard he tried to hide it. He didn't like my arrangement with Azrael. I just hoped that when Azrael turned down his request to join me back at the cave, he would keep his head.

Ethan was the calmest of us all, always had been, but when given a good reason to, he could be wildly unpredictable and quietly lethal. He didn't stand for anyone hurting those he loved, and I had always been one of those people. Even when I thought they'd all abandoned me after what happened to mom…

They hadn't.

They'd lived their lives to prove I wasn't insane, and to get revenge on the vampire who killed my mom and tried to kill me. They worked hard to find me. And finally, they had.

They never stopped being my friends. They never stopped loving me.

Good, I thought. Because I never stopped loving them, either. No matter how I hated to admit it. It was the reason why I never had anything more than one-night flings with guys I couldn't remember the names or faces of.

"Frost?" I hedged as Ethan tugged me further into the hall. "Please?"

It was the *please* that undid him. He could never say no to me. Now was no different than then. He huffed in defeat and uncrossed his arms. A muscle in his jaw twitched as he stalked after us, his heavy footfalls echoing in his wake.

"Fine. You want me? *You got me*," he said, his eyes flashing with wicked intent.

Oh yes. Come and get me big guy…

I let Ethan drag me the rest of the way into the corridor, but not before I tossed Blake a wink that I hoped conveyed both my thanks and my intent to have him once I was through with these two.

I yelped as Frost took me from Ethan's grip and swept me into one of the rooms. It was clearly Frost's bedroom. There was a king sized bed with rumpled sheets and blankets, and a low-lit lamp in the far corner casting a soft yellow glow over the plush dark green carpet the light oak nightstand, and matching dresser across the room.

There was really nothing at first glance that would tell me the room was his, but his heady scent was *all over it.* Warm leather and dried cloves with an undercurrent of tangy aftershave filled my nose and

I inhaled the scent deeply, instantly turned on even more.

"On the bed, woman," Frost ordered me.

I cocked my head at him, curious. Frost had surprised me before, on the other occasion where we'd fucked, he'd been submissive. Almost like he'd been afraid to take the lead. Maybe afraid he'd take it too far. Lose control. Maybe even hurt me.

He didn't seem too worried about that this time.

He needed to work out his frustrations and I would be happy to be his outlet.

But then he surprised me again as he turned to Ethan tilted his head towards the bed. "You too," he said.

Ethan didn't argue, climbing onto the bed behind me.

Frost didn't look like he was moving.

I quirked a brow at him.

"Take her, Ethan," Frost said, catching my wide-eyed gaze with a devious grin. "It's only fair I give you two a moment. Rose and I have had plenty."

Oh.

I gulped as I looked between Ethan and Frost.

He…he wanted to watch us first…

A burning began between my thighs and I barely concealed the flush that rose to my cheeks and prodded a small moan from my lips. The idea *really* turned me on. The little minx was purring loudly now, languidly stretching out her claws and cracking her neck in anticipation of a right good fucking by both of her guys.

Ethan, *sweet* Ethan, hovered just in front of me, his expression unsure. I could tell this wasn't Ethan's forte. Where I was sure Blake and Frost had a multitude of experience, I wasn't so sure about Ethan. But then again, I'd been wrong before. "Rose, are you sure you want this?"

My heart ached at the sincerity of the question and I had no doubt in my mind that if I said no, he would back away without question. But looking into his warm steeped tea eyes and drawing in a deep breath of his crisp nautical scent, I knew I was a goner. "*So* fucking sure," I breathed.

His eyes crinkled at the corners as he grinned, a dimple forming in his left cheek. I loved those dimples.

Frost parked himself in a low chair next to the closed door, leaning forward with his elbows resting on his knees, his hands steepled in front of his lips.

As Ethan's deft fingers undid the baggy jeans and tugged them off, Frost's gaze burned a hot path down my pelvis to the pulsating warmth of my pussy beneath my panties.

I let loose a small sound as Ethan tugged the jeans the rest of the way off and dropped them to the floor. Then he started with my sweater. He paused before he unclasped my bra, but only for a heartbeat, giving me another opportunity to back out.

Not a fucking chance.

As my breasts were set free, the nipples instantly pebbled and Ethan's jaw went slack as he took me in. His breaths deepened and he kept his eyes on my face as he hooked his fingers into my panties, pulling them off slowly. Once they were discarded and I was bared to them both, Ethan's eyes drew a curving path down my torso and fixated on the spot between my legs. He licked his lips.

Holy fucking shit.

"Your turn," I said, pushing myself up to a seated position. I undressed Ethan without the practiced grace he had in undressing me.

I stripped him with hungry, insistent fingers. After fiddling with the top button of his button down for far too long, I ended up tearing it from his body, the buttons scattering to the bed and floor. Ethan's brows raised, but he didn't complain as I pulled off his undershirt and exposed his smooth hairless chest. Not as buff as Frost, but his muscle was more defined. I ran my hand down the bumps of his abs and had his belt undone and removed in a blink.

Ethan moved to help me, kicking off his pants and briefs once I had them off.

He sprang free and I was left staring up at him in awe.

Why is it always the quiet nerdy ones with the biggest dicks?

Ethan must've seen my surprise because he winked down at me and began to kneel. Almost of their own accord, my hands moved forward, needing to feel the silky length of him to make sure what I was seeing was real.

No wonder Frost wanted to give me a minute with Ethan first. I wasn't sure I could handle them both inside me at the same time, not without easing into it. I stroked the satiny flesh of Ethan's cock and he trembled at my touch, his breath hitching.

"*Fuck*, Ethan," I breathed, my pussy wetting as I rubbed and tugged on him, bringing him to a full and rock-hard erection.

I caught Frost's gaze over Ethan's shoulder and saw that he had taken his own shirt off, and the top button of his jeans was now undone. His toes tapped against the carpet, counting down the minutes until he would allow himself to join.

Ethan reached his own hand down to my pussy and slid his fingers over my wet clit. I sucked in a breath and he growled, his fangs slipping free of his gums. His urge to feed was taking hold of him, but I could tell he had it controlled this time.

With all the blood in their fridge, I had to assume it was because he only recently fed.

I leaned in closer to him, wanting to feel the press of his lips. He obliged, kissing me deeply, his tongue delving into my mouth, hot and insistent as I continued my stroking of his cock and he continued his exploration of my pussy, dipping his fingers inside. I quivered in his embrace as my sex clenched around him.

Aroused, he moaned into my mouth and began to lay me down. "I'll take it slow," he whispered against my lips as he settled between my legs.

I wanted anything but slow, but after seeing the size of him for myself, I knew it was probably best to ease into it. Ethan stooped his head to circle a nipple with his hot tongue as he gently prodded at the wetness beneath my legs with the head of his cock.

My hands dove into his soft caramel hair, needing something to hold on to.

Out of the corner of my eye, I saw that Frost had stood and was now removing his pants. His own proud erection sprang free. He reached down and palmed it, stroking himself to make ready to join the fun. I wondered if I would blow him again, or if they'd both want inside of me at the same time. I wasn't opposed to anal, but I wasn't sure both of them would fit.

But fuck if I wasn't game to try.

Ethan brought my attention back to him as he bit my nipple gently, making my body jolt as he slid the tip of his cock into my pussy. I groaned at the pressure of him, feeling my body stretch to allow him inside. He eased back out and went a little further with the next thrust, shuddering as he did.

This wasn't Blake's bondage or Frost's hard and fast fucking; this was Ethan taking care of me. And I couldn't remember the last time anyone had done that. I surrendered to him, grinding my hips to tell him it was alright, that I was ready to feel the full force of him.

His mouth left my breast and he looked straight into my eyes as he sheathed himself inside of me. I gasped at the fullness, digging my nails into his back to keep myself from crying out too loudly.

Ethan bent low to kiss me again, tugging my bottom lip into his mouth to nibble on it. He began a slow and steady pace, our bodies molding together as though they were fucking *made* for each other.

He fit so fucking perfectly.

So beautifully.

"Ethan," I whimpered into his mouth as I felt my body beginning to crest the wave of my orgasm.

He maintained speed until I was heaving, my muscles coiled to brace for impact. My orgasm tore through me like a hot blade, and I clenched around him as wave after wave crashed over me. "That's it, my queen," he crooned, never breaking pace.

As I came out of the orgasm, he slowed, and the bed dipped near my feet. I blinked through the haze of my orgasm to see Frost kneeling on the bed behind Ethan.

"Flip her over," he told Ethan and my golden knight obliged, wrapping an arm under my lower back to lift my torso with one arm as he lifted my right leg with the other, spinning me on his cock until I was on my hands and knees with my fingers curled like talons into the bedsheets.

Fuck, he felt even *bigger* in this position. I had to adjust myself against him until I was more comfortable. I thought maybe Frost would slide under me, but as I turned back in anticipation of him coming, I saw him toss a small bottle away and stroke his erection with a substance that made it glisten in the low lighting.

Frost splayed his fingers over Ethan's back and my body tightened as I realized what he was about to do. He was going to fuck Ethan…while Ethan fucked me.

My inner lioness roared, and my knees trembled.

Ethan groaned as Frost entered him, and I felt his cock twitch inside of me. Holy fucking hell this was *hot*. I'd never been so turned on in my life.

Ethan began to move, plowing into me with a renewed vigor, each thrust into me also a pump on Frost's cock behind him. Ethan braced himself behind me with one hand on my right hip, but the other he snaked around to my front, his fingers finding my clit and beginning small, quick circular motions there.

I kept trying to look back, I wanted to see, but I was so lost in my own pleasure it was difficult not to focus all my attention on the glorious cock working its way in and out of my pussy. And Ethan's fingers as they rubbed me.

I caught a quick glance of them, though, in between waves of pleasure. Frost with his mammoth hands gripped firmly in the dip above Ethan's hips, his eyes shut in ecstasy as he fucked Ethan. His ripped chest gleaming with a layer of dewy sweat.

And Ethan, his face crumpling as he moaned at the dual sensation. His soft caramel hair falling forward to shield his eyes from me. The sight of them had the quickening sensation starting again and I cried out, moaning loudly as Ethan hurried to come with me and Frost fucked Ethan harder so he would join us, too.

Ethan's breaths hitched and I knew he was about to lose it. He came with a strangled moan, and the feel of his climax tipped both me and Frost over the ledge—sent us sprawling headfirst into orgasm. Frost roared, pumping into Ethan one last forceful time as Ethan thrust into me, his hand curling hard into my hip. Hard enough to bruise, but I didn't care.

I was doing my best not to scream from the force of my orgasm, bent low to bury my face in the pillow as racking tremors of delirium-inducing climax rushed through my body.

10

The room was tense with unspoken words when we were finally all together again in the living room. I'd popped off for a shower and a change of clothes. I was immeasurably grateful to find Ethan had thought to retrieve my bag from the burning wreckage of my truck, the big and beautiful Black Betty—*may her soul rest in peace.*

I wasn't surprised to see that the pack of cigarettes and lighter were missing. The fucker. Frost may not have said anything about it, but Ethan would have plenty to say if I lit up every time we fucked. Guess I would have to do away with that old tradition. I huffed. I could've really used one after that…

So, when I finally came out of the bathroom in a plume of steam, I was nicotine-free and clad in my hunting gear. My stretchy black pants and leather holster top with the bit that covered my scar —my loose-fitting leather jacket over top of it all. I even used a little of the men's hair product and a comb to tame the worst of the snags in my hair.

I didn't want to waste too much time, so I didn't bother with makeup or shaving. I didn't want to waste a single minute I had available to me to spend with my guys. But the shower had been necessary. After the ménage with Frost and Ethan, I'd been in dire need of one.

"You didn't need to do that," I grinned up at Blake as he set a tray down over my lap on the couch. While we were busy in the bedroom, he'd ordered me my old favorites. Chinese chicken fried rice, egg rolls, and those thin greasy noodles I liked to slather the red sweet and sour sauce on. A half-filled glass of what looked like whiskey rested in the corner.

"I did," he replied. "You look too pale. Is he not feeding you there?" Blake ground his teeth and I saw that same dangerous glimmer I'd seen in his eyes a thousand times before. He was *not* happy. I instantly wanted to reach out—to soothe him—but I knew he wouldn't want that, either.

"Yes. It's just—well, it's underground. It's like a cave. You know I don't do well in small spaces," I said, popping an enormous forkful of noodles in my mouth, moaning at the sweet and salty flavor.

"A cave?" Ethan asked from his seat beside me,

leaning forward to bend over his knees, his brows furrowing. I could see the gears and cogs in his mind turning. "And how long did you say it took for you to get here?"

I thought about it. I was asleep for most of the drive, but Azrael had said it would take about six hours, hadn't he? "Azrael said it was a six-hour drive."

His brows lowered even more, and he rose to go to the desk in the corner of the room and pushed the button on the tower to turn on the computer there. The three screens powered up and he began searching for more information.

"He's keeping you in a cave?" Frost growled, some of the malice making its way back into his expression and tightening his muscles. His face reddened. *Oh shit.* Azrael would be back to get me soon. I couldn't have him arriving to a raged-out Frost.

I winced. "Yeah, but it's not like a normal cave. It's really big. Even has an underground hot spring inside of it. And I have a room with a bed and a fireplace. And there's even a whole fucking *lab* in there. Like with hospital equipment and stuff."

Surprise won out over fury on Frost's face as he cocked his head at me. Then he grinned. I was confused as to why he was happy all of a sudden when Ethan said from the desk, "Got it."

Got what?

"You just gave us your location, Rosie," Frost said, smiling so big I could see teeth. He never smiled that big.

Blake even smirked, nodding at Ethan. "Well done," he said to Ethan.

I had been smiling along with them, but then reality set in. "It doesn't really matter," I told them. "I made a deal with him. And even all four of us together may not be a match for him. And besides, he has others there, too. I've only run into one, and I didn't leave him alive, but who knows how many other vampires he has in that place?"

"Plus, he can compel us," Blake said, frowning again.

I suddenly lost my appetite and set the tray down on the coffee table, but not before removing the glass of whiskey and taking a long swallow that burned all the way down to my belly. I grimaced. *Oh yes. I needed that.*

"Not if we get the jump on him," Frost interjected.

"Not worth the risk," I hissed. "I won't allow any of you fuckers to put yourself in danger over me. Not a goddamned chance."

Ethan moved into the living area, stepping around the thick central beam where a low fire burned in the electric fireplace. He crossed his arms over his chest and the bulge of his biceps beneath his elbow-length sleeved had my thighs squeezing in need of him all over again. I *really* hoped Azrael would let him come with us…

Ethan could provide a perfect distraction for me in my carved stone room. It was a big bed. I could share.

"Rose, it's really not your choice," he said, staring down at me apologetically. "We're going to fight for you just like you would fight for us."

My face fell. "You'll die, Ethan. All of you."

He inhaled deeply and inclined his head. "We might," he said quietly. "Or we might not."

Idiots. All of them. Thinking they could take on a fully mature *thousand-year-old* vampire. There was a line between confidence and stupidity, and they were getting dangerously close to crossing it.

There was one vital thing they all seemed to be forgetting though, and as much as I didn't want to stay in that fucking cave bent to Azrael's will, it made it bearable.

"What if Azrael is right?" I asked them, posing the question to Ethan since he was the one who agreed that what Azrael was trying to do could potentially work. "What if my blood can help vampires everywhere? What if it can cure you? Make you able to walk in sunlight again?"

Ethan's gaze darkened and Blake stalked back to the kitchen to pour himself a glass of whiskey, his jaw tight. They didn't like being tempted with it. I would bet they wanted to be able to see and feel the sun again more than almost anything else, except maybe not having to live off blood.

"I seriously fucking doubt that," Frost grumbled.

I rolled my eyes at him.

"I'm with Frost," Blake said, his smoky voice rolling over us from the kitchen.

"Yeah, well I agreed to be Azrael's test subject," I reminded them. "I'm not fucking happy about it, but I'm also not going to just dismiss the possibility because I don't believe it's possible. If I could give you guys back the sun…" I trailed off, my throat burning. "If I could take away your *thirst*…"

I didn't even know vampires existed until Mom told me when I was eight.

I didn't know I could compel, or that I was faster and stronger than any other human person I'd ever met until then, either.

I didn't know I was the last surviving Vocari until just *days* ago.

Anything is possible.

Ethan knelt in front of me, placing his hands on my knees, prompting me to look into his kind steeped-tea eyes. "You have to remember we *chose* this," he said, his expression pained. "I won't say there's a part of me that doesn't regret it, but our choices led us back to you."

"But Ethan—"

He shook his head, silencing me. "I'm not

disagreeing with you," he told me, and I heard both Blake and Frost growl on either side of us.

Ethan cut them each a look, daring them to speak against him in that quietly lethal way he had. "There *is* a chance that Azrael is right, and I *do* think it should be explored. But not at the expense of your freedom. Your safety."

I leaned forward and rested my forehead against his, breathing in deeply, allowing his smooth, crisp nautical scent to relieve some of the tension in my shoulders.

"What is it you're proposing?" Frost all but shouted, rising in a fury as he raked a hand through his hair. "That we just let her remain his *captive*?"

I hated this.

I wanted happy Frost back. The one who was waiting for me in my driveway with a devilish grin and open arms. I wanted the crease in Blake's forehead to go away and for darkness in Ethan's eyes to fade.

Ethan ground his teeth. "No, I'm not. What I'm saying it that maybe—"

"What?" Blake barked. "That fucker is going to be back here any minute and he's going to try to *take* her. What are we going to do about it?"

I gently removed Ethan's hands from my knees and stood, practically shaking with all the emotions my body was trying to contain. Fury. Fear. Frustration. Sadness.

"Stop," I said, my tone not leaving any room for argument. "Just fucking stop it. I'm going with Azrael and that's it. He said he would let me go when he was done with me."

I didn't mention the bit about how he didn't think I would survive long without his protection, afraid that may only cause them to worry more about things they couldn't control.

"And you trust him?" Blake sneered. His tone almost accusatory now.

I threw my hands up. "I don't really have a choice."

"But what if you did?" Ethan asked me with placid expression and monotone voice that gave away nothing.

What did he mean by that? What was he going to do?

My eyes widened and I was about to demand he explain what he meant when a loud buzzing came from the small intercom box by the door. My heart began to pound, and a cold sweat broke out over my chest.

Frost's fists clenched his gaze hardened.

"No," I warned him. "Get ahold of yourself."

That only seemed to make him angrier until I softened my tone. "Please," I asked more gently, and he deflated, though his face was still tinged red.

"You better have a plan," Frost muttered to

Ethan under his breath with a flicker in his eyes that spoke of murder.

For Ethan's sake, I hoped he did.

But for the sake of us all, I hoped they would see reason and just let me go.

Blake stalked over to the buzzer and hesitated, throwing me a fearful look that made my heart physically hurt. Blake was never afraid—of anything. He was the most battle hardened of us all. He had to be—living with the monster he had for a father had not only made him take an interest in professional fighting, callusing his exterior. It had also done something to him inside. Callusing his heart and mind, too.

Finally, Blake tore his gaze from me and jammed the button. We could all hear the door downstairs swing open and the slow, measured steps of Azrael as he ascended the stairs.

Each footfall made the weight on my chest grow. I was *not* looking forward to getting back in that coffin with him. Not one fucking bit.

I bit the inside of my cheek to keep myself in check. I didn't need to give away to the guys just how affected I was by all of this. I practiced slow breathing to steady my heartbeat, knowing they could hear it clear as day throbbing throughout the open space of the apartment.

The door opened and Azrael stepped inside.

11

I'd almost forgotten how he commanded attention from a room. The moment Azrael shut the door behind him, it was as though he'd sucked up all the air from the space, leaving it difficult to breathe. His vampiric energy made my skin bristle and the hairs on the back of my neck stand on end.

Azrael's detached expression shifted as he took us in, a growing anger clear in how he pressed his lips into a hard line. "I see," he said, as though we'd just had a conversation. I noticed then, how his eyes were fixed on Ethan's, and Ethan's on Azrael.

It *seemed* like they were having a conversation because *they were.* Ethan was speaking to Azrael from his mind.

And whatever he said was bad enough to shake Azrael's calm façade.

I didn't like this.

I really didn't fucking like this.

What had Ethan been saying to him?

"Ethan?" I hedged, my body tensing for a fight I knew I'd lose. I was so glad I had my stakes strapped to my thighs again, even if they were the shitty wooden ones. My hands twitched to grab them, but I didn't want to start something I couldn't finish. Maybe the katana would be better? I had it strapped across my back. Maybe it would be easier to behead him?

Nah. I still wasn't good enough with the katana to use it in an actual fight.

Azrael turned his attention to me, and the corners of his eyes drew down. "You just had to tell them..."

It took me a moment to understand what he was talking about.

I'd told them where Azrael's underground cave was. *Shit.*

I had my stakes drawn in half a second, but it was too late. Before I could even lunge for him, Azrael was a blur of movement in the apartment. A blow to my chest sent me sprawling backward until I was crashing into and over the back of the couch, rolling until I was a heap on the plush carpet, my back aching from the impact.

I was back on my feet in seconds and I gasped at what I found in the entryway. Blake, Ethan, and

Frost surrounding Azrael, each in a different fighting stance—but *all* frozen. Completely unable to move. And Azrael, grinning wickedly at them as though they were mice caught in his trap.

"Azrael," I croaked, barely able to breathe. "Please..."

No. No. *No.* This was my fault. *The fucker can read minds, Rose!* What did you think would happen after you led them to his secret lair?

Stupid!

We stood like that for what seemed an age, both of us locked onto each other's gazes, neither moving an inch. And all the while my guys stood like sentinel gargoyles, as though carved from stone. The only indication that they were alive the burning fires in each of their eyes.

Azrael sighed deeply and peeled his eyes from mine, seeming to decide something. I held my breath, deciding in that moment that if he killed them, I'd attack, and I wouldn't stop until one of us was dead.

I readied myself for the fight of my life, clenching my jaw, my hands tightening on my stakes. Ready to charge.

"You will forget where my dwelling is," Azrael said instead, and I let the breath I'd been holding leak out between my lips. "You will not look for it. Even if Rose tells you where it is, you will not hear it. You don't know where I'm keeping Rose and you'll *never* find it."

Straightening his jacket, Azrael cracked his neck and shuddered. "Now," he said, in a calmer tone, his sights set on Ethan. "We were discussing your proposal…?"

Holy shit.

I knew when Azrael released his hold on them because they all sort of *relaxed.* Just a little—a slight lowering of the shoulders and bending of the spine.

"Will you agree to it?" Ethan asked as though nothing in the last few minutes had even happened. Frost and Blake seemed confused and stepped back from Azrael, glancing around—likely trying to figure out why they were standing so close all of a sudden.

They'd put it together any second now.

Blake spotted me in the living area, breathing hard, my hair a mess from tumbling over the couch. "Rose? What are you doing over there?"

"How did she—" Frost started, but cut himself off, turning back to Azrael with a renewed fury. "What did you do?" he roared at the older vampire. "Why did you compel us?"

Azrael waved his hand as though to wordlessly say '*oh, nothing to worry about.*'

"Frost," I said, swallowing, my eyes fixed on Azrael who was silently daring me to give him a reason to cut them all down. "It's not important. Leave it."

Frost stepped another couple feet back from Azrael, and I thanked whatever stroke of luck made him listen to me. I went to join him and reached down to take his hand, surprised when he held mine back. Frost wasn't the type to show affection in front of someone he didn't know.

"In answer to your request," Azrael resumed his conversation with Ethan. "I'll...*consider it...if* she cooperates."

Ethan turned to me and winked.

I was so confused. "And my *other* request?"

Azrael pursed his lips, considering Ethan the way a physicist might consider a particularly difficult math equation. "I'll allow it," he said finally. "But if you cross me..."

"Yeah, I get it," Ethan said, nodding. "You'll kill me."

"Maybe," Azrael replied. "Though I am also fond of *other* forms of punishment. Lobotomy has its charm, for instance. But then, so does the complete and utter shattering of a mind—forcing someone to relive their darkest moment over and over again until they end it themselves."

My stomach soured.

He could do that?

I wasn't sure why I was surprised, but the thought of him doing *any* of those things to my guys sent my heart slamming in my ribcage and my blood rushing in my ears. Frost's grip on my hand tightened.

"What's going on?" I asked, stepping away from the warmth and comfort of Frost.

"Ethan was just filling me on his very interesting line of work," Azrael mused. "I could use someone with his…*expertise*."

Blake glared at Ethan, his knuckles bone white. "What did you do?" he hissed at Ethan.

Ethan didn't even glance in Blake's direction, instead he turned to offer me a half-hearted smirk and lifted one shoulder in a shrug. "Looks like you're stuck with me," he said, and his smile broadened.

12

After Ethan explained to the guys to move all of his appointments and rushed to fill a bag with a few of his things, we were ready to go.

I still couldn't believe Ethan was actually coming with us. I was both utterly relieved and so fucking scared and pissed at him for putting himself in the line of fire for me. I had no doubt in my mind that if Ethan stepped out of line or even attempted to attack Azrael in his own home that the older vamp would dispose of him.

I'd seen the way he ended the vampire that attacked me in the corridor just the day before. He was without remorse. And he'd acted so fast I wasn't even sure if he'd thought it through or had just went for the throat.

I shivered at the thought.

At least Ethan was the most level-headed of us.

So long as he behaved himself and did as Azrael said, maybe both of us could get out of this alive.

The other guys, however, were far from pleased with the situation. Now, not only was Azrael taking me with him to a place they would now *never* be able to find, but he was also taking Ethan.

"When will you bring them back?" Blake asked, his voice gruff and gray eyes flashing in the moonlight on the stoop. His hand tightened on my shoulder and I had a feeling I would need to pry myself free if I was going to be able to leave.

Azrael paused midway across the road and turned, considering. His gaze flicked to Ethan and something in Ethan's eyes told me he'd already spoken to Azrael about this, just in a way that only Azrael could hear. I would have to ask him what the fuck they were talking about and why he was leaving the rest of us in the dark when we got there. "Depends," Azrael responded. "Maybe a week. Maybe a month…"

"That's not good enough," Frost growled, his white blond hair glinting in the moonlight.

Azrael, unperturbed, leveled his icy gaze on Frost. "It depends on *them*," he told Frost, inclining his head in the direction of Ethan and me. "So long as I get what I need, I see no reason I can't agree to your *friend's* joint-custody arrangement."

Ethan's what?

"But that's *only* if I get what I need."

Were they talking about…about *sharing* me? Like I was goods to be traded and haggled over?

Men…

I sighed, but I wasn't about to complain. A *joint-custody arrangement* was more than I'd dared to hope for.

I could be a good little girl, couldn't I? I glanced at the smug face of Azrael and almost snarled. It wouldn't be easy, that was for sure.

Azrael didn't wait to answer any more questions, he continued across the road to the waiting hearse on the other side. "Time to go," he called back and I stiffened under Blake's grasp, turning to bury my face in his chest.

I inhaled his clean linen and suede scent—the hint of vanilla bringing me a measure of peace. He wrapped his arms around me tightly. "Come back to us," he whispered in my hair. "*Soon* or I might go mad."

I tilted my head up to find him glaring down into my eyes, the gray of his irises near black—his jaw set and his lips in a firm line. I went up on tip toe and kissed him. He stiffened for a moment before he kissed me back. "I will," I promised.

He fixed me with a sad smile.

"And when I do, you can tie me up however you like," I added with a wink and lick of my lips.

I felt Blake's cock twitch beneath his jeans and

was glad to find that some of the creasing in his forehead had lessened.

Then I turned to Frost, who was growling instructions at Ethan, his voice low.

Ethan was nodding and then stepped away from Frost to speak with Blake.

I took his place in front of Frost and opened my arms. “Come here, big guy,” I said with my best smile.

Frost grunted, but did as I requested, wrapping me up in his huge, warm embrace. He nuzzled into my hair, breathing deeply. His leather and clove scent enveloped me, and it was *so* hard to let go. When I did, Frost placed two fingers beneath my chin and lifted my face to him. He kissed me swiftly and then pulled away, staring intently at me with his bright green eyes. “Be careful, Rosie.”

I nodded and Frost gritted his teeth as he released me. “Now go before I lose it,” he added, and I could see by how his face reddened, that he was far from joking.

I stepped back two feet and grabbed Ethan by the elbow, cutting his conversation with Blake short. “Come on,” I told Ethan. “We have to go.”

Seeing the reason why, Ethan nodded and stepped away. “If I have anything to do with it,” he said to the other two of our puzzle of four. “We’ll be back sooner than you think.”

“Go,” Frost ground out, and Blake moved into a

cautionary position halfway in front of him…just in case.

"Come on, man," Blake was saying to Frost as we finally turned away. "Let's go inside. I don't know about you, but I could use a drink."

Ethan took my hand as we followed Azrael over to the back of the hearse where the compelled driver was waiting. As I heard the door shut on a still seething Frost across the street, I remembered something. I glanced up at the sky. I had no idea what time it was, but I knew for certain the sun would rise in less than six hours.

"So, how are we going to do this?" I asked Azrael. "There's only one coffin."

"I suppose I get to snuggle with your mate, then," he replied. "Since you're the only one immune to sunlight."

I cocked my head at him, confused for a moment before he stepped in and locked eyes on me. "Sleep," he commanded, and I felt my eyelids flutter and my legs buckle beneath me. I tried to fight it, but it was no use, my body sagged under the immense pressure of his compulsion. The last thing I heard before I fell into strong arms and the scents of white birch and rain filled my nose was Ethan cursing.

When I awoke, I found myself in the front seat of

the hearse, next to an empty driver's seat. My mouth was dry as hell and there was a gooey substance in the corners of my eyes. I wiped the corner of my mouth and the back of my hand came away slick with drool.

Ugh.

Nasty.

"I'm glad to see you had a nice rest," a voice said from the open window next to me. I jumped and turned, trying to draw a stake from between my legs with clumsy fingers.

"Fuck!" I exclaimed, blinking as my vision and mind focused, remembering where I was and what had happened. I let go of the tight breath in a sigh and set my stake back down in my lap. "You compelled me," I said accusingly to Azrael, shoving open the passenger side door to make him move out of the way as I stretched out my back. It was sore from my Katana pressing into it the whole drive. "Stop doing that," I growled.

Azrael's brows raised. "I don't enjoy it," he replied, deadpan as I stepped out of the vehicle. He waved an arm toward where Ethan was standing next to the coffin, examining his surroundings. "However, I think you'll find the reward equal to the price."

I grinned and went to Ethan, catching him by surprise with a tackle hug. He was really here.

Yeah, a prisoner in this fucking cave with you, the more rational part of me chided. *Good job, Rose.*

I told that part to take a hike and enjoyed the moment.

"Hey," Ethan whispered, kissing the top of my head before maneuvering me to stand at his side with his arm around me. He nodded to Azrael. "Thank you," he said, and I could tell it took a great deal of restraint to eek out those two words. "For allowing me to accompany her."

"Don't make me regret it," Azrael replied, his eyes darkening. With a snap of his fingers the woman who'd tended me in my room appeared out of one of the darkened channels across the cavern and curtseyed to her master.

"Take Rose back to her chamber and see that she's well fed. I'll be needing her in the lab within the hour."

I gulped, clutching tighter to Ethan.

Ethan rubbed some warmth back into my arm and looked between the woman and Azrael. "May I go with her?"

"No," Azrael said plainly. "You will accompany me to the lab."

Ethan's jaw twitched, but he did not argue. "As you wish."

Azrael regarded Ethan a peculiar look, as though measuring his sincerity and perhaps liking what he saw. It made my skin crawl and I shuddered.

My inner lioness roared, *back the fuck off! He's mine.*

Azrael inclined his head to my golden knight. "Hmmmm," he said, the sound low and throaty. "I think we'll get along after all."

13

Though the first few bites were difficult to get down, I managed to finish the entire tray of lavish food. Chicken in a peppery cream sauce with fresh bread and a small mountain of steamed vegetables. The woman, whose name I learned was Estelle, had sat in the chair by the fire and watched me consume the entire thing.

Azrael had said to be sure I got something to eat and it seemed she took her orders *very* seriously. I wondered how many times he'd compelled her? If her mind was even her own anymore or if she was just an empty, dried husk of the woman she used to be.

It was sad, really. With her round red cheeks, kind eyes, and occasionally saucy attitude, I thought she would make a great auntie or grandmother.

"Do you have any family?" I hedged as I

polished off the last bite of the bread and refilled my water glass.

Her eyes narrowed. "No."

"None at all?"

Her mouth tightened, deepening the wrinkles around her chin and cheeks. "Are you quite finished?" she snapped, rising from the seat to remove the tray from my bed.

Yeah, I wasn't going to get anywhere with this one. She had very likely been compelled to forget her previous life. I'd seen it done before, though mostly the tactic was used to create human blood slaves. A vampire would erase all of their memories and implant new ones for them. Telling them that their only purpose in life was to be a blood-bag for their master. In those cases, only the vampire who placed the compulsion on the slave could remove it.

I couldn't help Estelle. Even if I were strong enough to battle against Azrael's compulsion.

Not strong enough *yet*, I corrected the thought. If what Azrael said was true about my mother—that her compulsion had been stronger than Azrael's brother's, then I supposed one day it would be possible.

I just had to survive long enough.

I snorted. *Yeah, right.* There was a reason no one in the entire history of our family had ever lived past forty…

"Up with you," Estelle said as she collected the

crumbs from my bed onto the tray. "The master waits for no one."

"Yeah," I scoffed. "I noticed."

Like a good little Rose, I followed Estelle through the stone corridors, this time committing every turn to memory. If I did it every time she took me out of the room, eventually I would have the place figured out. That way if Azrael didn't keep his word in the end, I would at least stand a chance at finding my own way out.

I knew we were coming up on the lab as the appearance of artificial light began to brighten the stone around us, and then eventually, I could see the opening that would lead us inside. I clenched my jaw, nervous. Would he be making vamps feed off me? Or would he just be extracting some of my blood to test on? I seriously hoped it was the latter.

The idea of letting any vamp outside of my guys feed off me made me feel instantly disgusted and my stomach rolled.

Estelle showed me inside and then without a word vanished back the way she'd come.

The lab was bustling with activity—a much different sight to when Azrael first brought me here to set the bones in my leg. Azrael and Ethan were speaking near a bank of monitors along the far wall. Azrael caught sight of me out of the corner of his eye, but didn't pause his conversation.

There were three others in the lab now, too. All

of them *human* if I wasn't mistaken. I couldn't feel their energies. The two men and one woman wore lab coats and blue latex gloves as they made ready for my arrival. Each had that glazed look in their eyes as they worked, telling me they'd all been compelled.

My fury spiked and I had to clench my fists to keep myself from drawing my stakes. I set my sights on Azrael as he finished his conversation with Ethan, even going so far as to pat him on the shoulder as he turned to me.

I didn't like to see him touching Ethan. I immediately wanted to break his hands and pull Ethan away, but I stopped myself.

"Thought you didn't like compelling people," I said through clenched teeth as Azrael and Ethan approached.

"I don't."

My gaze flitted to the three humans in the lab. "Doesn't fucking look like it…"

"Does she ever stop cursing?" Azrael posed the question to Ethan with a raised brow.

Ethan shrugged. "No. Afraid you'll just have to get used to it."

Azrael held out a hand to me. "Come," he said, not a command, but a request. A test to see if I would obey.

My stomach soured as I placed my hand in his. I almost gagged as he wrapped his long fingers around my hand and tugged me toward what looked like a gurney. His hand was ice cold and smooth, like worn leather. The fucker didn't even *feel* like a living being. He felt like what he was—a monster.

"Sit," Azrael gestured to the gurney and I was all too eager to let go of his hand so I sat, positioning myself in the middle of the slim cushion.

"Now what?" I demanded, eyeing the doctors or scientists or whoever they were. My heart ached for them.

Before Azrael could answer me, I blurted, "Are you going to let these people go after you're through with them or are you going to turn them into blood slaves?" My hands gripped the gurney with knuckles as I waited for his response.

I couldn't just sit here and not say anything. How could Ethan? I glanced at him with pain-filled eyes. His expression was without feeling, and I wondered what he was thinking behind the mask of calm he wore. Seeing my distress, however, he reached out and put a steadying hand on my shoulder.

Still, I couldn't relax. "Well?" I demanded, glaring up into Azrael's mismatched eyes again.

He looked more severe with his long brown hair tied back with a strip of leather at the nape of his neck. Somehow it made his cheekbones seem sharper and his jawline stronger. His eyes flashed as he seemed to contemplate a response. His lips pursed. "I won't make them blood slaves," he offered, not giving me any other insight into his insidious plans.

"Will you kill them, then?"

"No."

I groaned at his inability to answer a question properly. All I seemed to ever get from him were half-truths and partial answers. It was getting old already.

"Satisfied?" He asked, clasping his hands behind his back, making his chest seem wider.

"Hardly," I grumbled, but it wasn't like I could do anything about it. "Let's just get this over with."

Azrael lifted a hand to signal the humans in the room and they began to wheel over trays of equipment and put masks on their faces.

I focused on Ethan as the people formed a ring around me. Although there was a crease of worry between his brows, he looked…fascinated. This was his element, I realized. It was a place like this—well, not in a cave—where he might've eventually worked if he hadn't turned himself.

Now, I could see the strain in the muscles in his neck and how he moved an extra foot back from the humans as they began cleaning a spot at the crease of my elbow. He twitched and his chest stopped moving.

Frost said he had the most difficult time with

control. I hoped his most recent feeding was still enough to keep him from doing anything he might regret.

"You don't have to stay in here," I told him as one of the humans jabbed a needle into my skin and bright red liquid began pumping out of my body and into a bag.

Ethan shook his head. "I'm staying."

Azrael lifted a brow at the pair of us but said nothing. He would likely get all the information he needed from both mine and Ethan's thoughts.

As my blood drained out of me, another of the doctors pulled out a pair of scissors and cut a small bit of hair from my head. The third doctor person, a woman, drew yet another pair of scissors and when I realized what she was about to do, I all but jumped from the table. "Whoa," I said, craning my neck to Azrael. "Why's she trying to cut off my clothes?"

These were my hunting leathers. There was not a damned chance I was letting anybody at them with scissors, deal or not.

"Bone marrow sample," Azrael explained without emotion. "They need access to your back to extract it.

"Bone…what?"

Ethan's brows lowered. "You didn't say anything about needing a marrow sample," Ethan said to

Azrael, his tone accusatory and his face growing pale.

"Didn't I?" Azrael replied offhandedly.

"Well they aren't cutting off my clothes," I said. "Do you have like a hospital gown or something I can change into?"

Azrael lips pressed together. "Afraid not. It wasn't high on my list of priorities."

Dick.

I unzipped the top part of my top and undid the clasps, glad I was wearing a bra beneath it. I pulled off the whole top and handed it to Ethan, who's ears tinged pink as the sight of me without a shirt. I shook my head at him. It was only hours ago that he'd fucked me with that incredible mammoth cock of his while Frost fucked him from behind. My pussy tightened at the still-fresh memory, and I smiled at him. Even now he averted his gaze, always the gentleman.

I loved that about him.

Azrael, however, seemed less like he cared about my state of nudity. He watched as I sat back down and listened to the doctor's gentle prodding as they asked me to lay on my side facing Azrael and Ethan.

Something cold was painted onto my back and I shivered, reaching out to hold on to the metal rail.

Ethan's face turned a shade of green as he looked away, his entire body going rigid. I wondered for a fraction of a second why he seemed to be so distraught before they rammed something big and sharp into my back. It knocked the breath out of me and my hands tightened on the metal rail. My body tried to shy away from the pain, but the two other doctors held me firmly in place.

Stars exploded behind my eyelids as whatever horrid tool they were using broke through bone, puncturing my spine.

"*Fuck*," I cursed.

"Try not to move," Azrael said, his tone indifferent. "One wrong move here could turn you into a vegetable."

I let loose a string of curses that would have had the devil blushing, my body shaking as my nerve-endings screamed from the pain. A warm hand brought me out of the momentary misery and I glanced up to see Ethan, pale and pained himself from being this close to so much human blood, but somehow, he had a small, reassuring smile on his lips. "It's almost over," he told me, and I felt the thick needle retracting from my back.

My body slumped as it exited my flesh and I bit back the urge to barf as I felt warm liquid roll out from the puncture mark and down to the gurney.

I really hoped it was just blood and not some weird fluid. Blood I could deal with. Hell, I'd spilled more of it than any known serial killer in the world. But there was something about *other* fluids that grossed me the fuck out.

"That's all for today," Azrael announced as the human doctors patched me up. The pain receded quickly as my body began its natural healing process.

I sat back up as the doctors moved away and sighed. *That wasn't so bad,* I thought to myself.

The following days had me second guessing my choices.

They passed with more of the same. Drawing blood. More marrow and hair samples. Some swabs of saliva. Skin samples. I drew the line at removing a tooth. No way was I going to walk around with a missing tooth for the rest of life. I was sure my body would reject a dental implant, so that was a major no-go.

Azrael started keeping me in the lab for most of each day. He even began testing me in other ways. Testing my mental barriers. He would ask me to try to resist his compulsion. So far, I'd hadn't ever been able to. Then he would ask me to try to compel him. Other than a pinched face, Azrael showed no signs of strain in resisting me.

He tested my stamina one day by having a treadmill brought in and hooking me up to a bunch of monitors that showed symbols and numbers I didn't understand. I lasted on full speed for six hours straight.

My legs and core ached for the next three days.

Ethan was my constant companion in the lab, but to my complete and utter disappointment, Azrael wouldn't allow him back to my chambers with me. He didn't say as much, but I suspected it was because he didn't trust Ethan not to feed from me.

Whether because he wanted to keep my blood untainted by vampire venom, or because he was afraid Ethan wouldn't be able to stop and he'd lose his lab-rat, I wasn't sure.

"You best get some sleep, dear," Estelle said as she folded the dirty bedding into her arms and rose to her full height.

"Can I have a bath?" I hedged. My body was still a bit sore from stamina-testing-day and there was dried blood on my back and arms from where they did more marrow and skin samples today.

Estelle frowned. "I wouldn't want to mess your clean sheets," I added, knowing she couldn't refuse. If there was anything I'd learned about Estelle this past week, it was that she *hated* finding my bedding dirty with dried blood or stinking with sweat. She changed them almost every day now.

It'd been almost three days since my last bath, though it was always hard to tell the passage of time in this godforsaken place. I'd slept twice since my last bath, so I had to assume it was close to three days now, since my eyelids were droopy, and it was almost time for me to go to bed.

Maybe I'd try to barter for a clock from Azrael tomorrow…

I'd already traded a new truck for some extra skin samples. Azrael had easily agreed to provide me with a shiny new Black Betty once he was finished with his experiments. No truck on this planet could replace *my* Betty, but I would need a vehicle if I ever got out of here. And if memory served correct, my Betty was beyond repair.

"Oh, very well," Estelle grumbled. "Come on, then, follow me."

"I know the way," I replied, pushing my sweat-dampened black hair away from my face as I rose from the bed.

Estelle's small eyes narrowed and her plump face pinched, suspicious. "All the same," she said. "It's my duty to see you don't get lost."

By the way she said it, I knew her true meaning was something more akin to; *It's my duty to see you don't somehow manage to find your way out…*

"Can't have you wanderin' on your lonesome."

I shook my head and rolled my eyes to the heavens. I didn't bother responding, I just followed my stout chambermaid into the chilly corridor and through the winding passages until the distinct scents of sulfur and damp stone filled my nostrils and the kiss of warm steam brushed its lips against my bare arms.

"Here we are," Estelle said. "Back for you in an hour."

"Thanks," I offered.

She whipped her head around as though she'd been slapped. Her eyes widened.

Estelle pursed her lips. "So, it *does* know it's manners," she teased.

I rolled my eyes. "Don't get used to it."

I waited until I could no longer hear her footfalls in the corridor over the sound of the rushing water. "Ethan?" I whispered into the steam.

Strong arms pinned me from behind and I barely had enough time to hold my breath before we splashed into the hot water. It closed over my head and I elbowed my attacker in the ribs. His arms came loose, and I spun beneath the water, ready to pull him into a headlock between my legs. But he put a hand beneath my arse and pushed us both back up to the surface.

His golden hair was closer to chocolate from being wet, but even in the steam covered dark I knew that face. I splashed him, my cheeks flaming. "I almost drowned you," I chided him.

Ethan laughed. I hadn't heard that sound in so long that it pulled at something in my chest. I moved in and placed a hand over his mouth. "Quiet or someone'll hear us," I hissed into his ear.

We'd discussed meeting here earlier in the lab, in a rare moment when Azrael had left to see to something else. I could hardly believe we'd pulled it off.

I was sure one of us would crack and think about it when he returned—alerting him to our plan, but it seemed we'd actually managed to get away with it.

And thank fuck because if I had to watch Ethan in that lab for another day without being able to touch him how I wanted to, I was sure I would explode.

It had been incredible to see him so in his element. He worked alongside the doctors and scientists. Conversed with Azrael. I even noticed he had begun running some of his own tests. He never asked me for samples of his own. I could tell it bothered him greatly that I had to be poked and prodded daily, but it seemed Azrael wasn't opposed to Ethan stealing small bits of the samples that were already taken from me.

I didn't like the way Azrael watched Ethan, though. There was something sinister about it. He watched him like a bird of prey would a field mouse. *If* Azrael ever let us go back to see the guys, I would be asking Ethan to remain behind with them when I returned. I didn't trust that Azrael wouldn't hurt Ethan.

I would be fine. Azrael needed me. But Ethan? He was disposable.

"How did you convince Ms. Crankypants to let you out of your cell?" Ethan asked jokingly, pulling me into his arms. I was surprised to find he was already naked, and his body was smooth from the minerals in the water. My hands slid around his shoulders to his back as though he was covered in a fine layer of silk.

I gulped. My stomach flipped as his cock brushed against my inner thigh, still soft, but starting to harden.

"She isn't so bad," I replied in a whisper, surprised at the swiftness of the response. Estelle truly was starting to grow on me.

Ethan lifted my feet from the stone floor beneath the water and hefted me into his arms, carrying me further into the dark—deeper into the steam and nearer the small waterfall so we wouldn't be overheard.

Smart man.

Ethan set me down and guided me backward. I could just make out the shape of him, but nothing else. The steam here was too thick and the darkness too rich. When my back met a section of smooth, warm rock, he stopped.

"I didn't think I'd get to touch you again until we went home," Ethan whispered as he leaned into me.

He kissed and nibbled at the nape of my neck.

I shivered.

His hands moved to unzip my top and remove it, followed by my pants, bra, and panties. All the while he dropped kisses along my neck, up and down either side until I was burning with the need to be touched.

I didn't care that my clothes were probably lost forever in the spring. When his cock brushed against my clit, I almost cried out. Ethan clamped a hand over my mouth to stifle the sound.

"Shhhh," he whispered into my ear.

I nodded against his warm, wet, palm.

When he moved his hand away, I all but lurched forward, pressing my lips to his. Ethan's hand moved to cup the back of my head and his body pressed in flush against mine, forcing my back hard against the wall beneath the water. His erection was long and hard now against my belly and I moaned against his mouth. He used the opportunity to slip his tongue inside and claim my mouth.

I reached between us to take his silky cock into my hand. Ethan shuddered at the contact and his fangs slid low, piercing my lower lip. A rush of sensation rippled through me as the tiny amount of venom entered my bloodstream. My back arched and I clutched him to me. Blood trickled from the small wound and Ethan slid his tongue over it, his fingers pressing *hard* where they held my hips against the wall.

His body froze as he swallowed me down and

my own body rebelled. *No.* I didn't want him to stop. *Hell, no.*

I slid my hand back and forth over his cock, and he purred, his body tensing and relaxing all at once. "Rose," he hissed between clenched teeth. "I… can't."

"*Oh yes you can,*" I commanded. "You won't hurt me."

He shook his head.

"You *won't.*"

Suddenly, I wanted more than just his cock inside of me. I wanted his fangs with a desire that bordered on being frantic. My body had gotten a small taste and it was hungry for more.

Starving.

And I *knew* he felt the same. Now that he'd tasted me, I knew he craved more, too.

"Take me," I told him. "I want you to take me."

I tipped my head to one side and bared my neck to him.

He hissed.

I pulled him closer, closing my eyes in anticipation.

Ethan didn't disappoint. But unlike when Frost gave in with a feral thirst and tore into my carotid, Ethan moved with slow, practiced movements, as though proving to himself he could maintain restraint.

When his breath caressed the spot beneath my

ear, goosebumps pricked my skin and I shivered again, my breaths low and slow while I waited.

He took me into his mouth gently, and it was only when I felt his lips against me that he finally pushed the sharp points of his fangs into my flesh. I stopped breathing, not wanting to make any pained sounds and scare him off. But as the pain ricocheted up my neck, I couldn't help a few involuntary twitches.

And then it was already fading. The pain was evaporating as surely as all the hot steam surrounding us. My body came alive under the water as Ethan's venom did its work. I snaked my hand around the back of his neck and held him tightly to me. He responded in kind, biting down harder, making my body buck against him.

As my hips pressed forward, I felt the brush of his cock again and was ravenous for another reason. Ethan, understanding what I wanted, reached down to touch me. His fingers burned a trail down my chest, stopping briefly to cup my breasts and tease my nipples until they were pebbled and aching beneath the water.

Lower until they brushed against my opening, teasing as they probed the area with slow strokes.

Ethan readjusted his stance and I realized what he was going to do only a millisecond before he did it. Once he felt how slick I was with my own silky wetness, and how the warm water had loosened me enough to take him in, he thrusted.

His fingers moved to my thigh, lifting it to the side to open me up to him. Then he was inside me. This time it wasn't gentle. This time he didn't inch his way in. This time he drove his delicious cock into me until I was gasping, my body clamoring to adjust to the length and girth of him. The feeling of fullness was so blissfully absolute that I had to stifle a shout.

Ethan moved his hand from my cheek to cover my mouth again, and as he drew out of me, I moaned into his slick palm and as he drove back in I cried out, but the sound was muffled.

My head swam and I couldn't be sure whether it was from the waves of pleasure cascading over me, dragging me beneath their undulating surface, or because he'd taken too much blood.

I didn't really fucking care.

I lifted my other leg from the ground so he was effectively pinning me against the stone wall with his cock and his fangs. Oh yes. This was fucking bliss.

I closed my eyes to quell the dizziness and ground my hips against him. Ethan obliged with slow thrusts, pausing to grind his hilt against my clit with each one.

My breasts brushed against his chest and his hand covering my mouth tightened. The one gripping my thigh dug in so hard I thought he might break skin. With my head still floating somewhere in the air and my body still victim to his venom, I whimpered against Ethan's palm. My heart drove a single hard beat against my chest and then skittered into several soft beats before it beat hard and slow again.

My head lolled back and in a moment of clarity, I whispered, "Ethan…stop…"

I couldn't be sure if he heard me over the crashing of water into the spring. Hell, I couldn't be sure if any sound escaped my lips at all, but I'd certainly meant to say it.

His fangs dug deeper still into my neck and a sound somewhere between a growl and a pained moan reverberated in his chest.

"Eth—"

I didn't even get his full name out before he retracted his fangs and as my vision began to clear and his bite began to heal, I saw his face, horrified, cheeks flushed with his fresh feed. Blood staining a spot on his lower lip.

"Rose—" he started, but as the dizziness began to subside, I hushed him with a finger to his lips. With his venom still flowing in my veins and his cock still lodged deep into my pussy, I couldn't have him backing down.

I wiped the blood from his lower lip and drew him in closer, staring into his eyes as I clenched my pussy around his cock. "Finish what you started," I told him with a grin, my heartbeat leveling back out.

"I almost—"

"You did better than Frost did," I retorted. It wasn't entirely true. I didn't think either one did better than the other, but Ethan could use the boost to his confidence.

He shook his head at me, but some of the worry had left his face. *Good.*

"Is that so," he replied with a gleam in his light brown eyes, his hands going beneath the water to circled around my hips until he was holding me up by my thighs.

I nodded. "Now, I need you to fuck me good and hard. I don't know when we'll get another chance and it's all I can think about watching you work in the lab…"

He bent down and stole a kiss from my lips. A hard, fast kiss that had my belly flipping low and hard.

"As you wish," he said when he pulled away and locked onto my thighs.

His cock pushed into me, driving my lower back into the stone. He fucked me hard and fast, all the while watching me through the mist. He liked to see the effect he was having on me. And much as I tried to stay quiet, I couldn't help the low moans tearing from my throat, or the cry of passion when my release exploded through my body and left me shuddering against both Ethan and the stone.

"That's it," Ethan said, but by the look on his face, I knew he was far from stopping.

Once my orgasm was finished, he pulled out and I ached from the loss of him. I opened my mouth to protest, but he kissed me again, rough and passionate before he lifted me and spun me around to face the wall. I planted my hands against the stone as he nudged his cock between my cheeks.

He hesitated, but I rubbed my ass against his cock, telling him without the need for words that I wanted him there, too.

With a groan, Ethan worked his tip into my ass as his fingers circled my thigh to find my silky clit. He rubbed me as he entered me from behind and the dual sensation had me biting hard on my lower lip to stop the sounds of pleasure and pain from tumbling out.

My fingernails bit down into the stone as he entered me fully. I gasped and arched my back. Ethan moaned as he began pumping into me, his body tense and straining.

"Fuck," he hissed, in a rare curse. "You're so tight, Rose."

I knew he was close, and the knowledge sent me spiraling to my own release once more.

His fingers rubbed and rubbed, slipping back and forth over the pebble of my clit until I was near screaming. That combined with the rhythmic pumping of his cock and the hard grip of his hand on my side would have me undone in seconds.

Ethan fucked me harder, his fingers frantic now, urging me to come with him. Begging me. The quickening began low in my belly and I held my breath as it hit a mind-bending apex, pitching both of us from the ledge to fall into the silken black abyss in a heap of gasping breaths, hardened muscle, and shaking moans.

14

We were a pair of giggling fools when we finally found our way out of the hot spring, even though I sensed Ethan's bliss was dampened by the fact that he nearly lost control. I hoped he wouldn't be too hard on himself. He *did* manage to stop himself, after all.

Wasn't that something?

I got the distinct feeling I shouldn't bring it up just yet, though. He was taut as a bowstring and trying hard to hide it from me. Wouldn't want to ruin all his hard work. Let him think he had me fooled, just this once, if it made him feel better and gave him the time he needed to process.

Estelle hadn't returned to collect me yet, so we bathed together in the cooler waters near the entrance. Ethan brushed the tangles from my hair beneath the water, and soaped my back and chest, his gaze scrutinizing as he checked me for injury.

"I'm not hurt," I offered in a whisper as he finished soaking the suds from the tops of my breasts.

He pressed his lips together and nodded.

I knew it was all I would get from him.

I was so busy analyzing him that I didn't hear Estelle coming down the corridor. So, it was a good thing Ethan did. He vanished beneath the dark water in the blink of an eye as the echo of Estelle's footfalls grew louder.

"I hope you're good and washed, girl. The master has asked to see you."

My brows furrowed. I'd only just left the lab a couple of hours before. What could he possibly want now?

"But why—"

"I don't pretend to know the master's mind, Rose."

I thought it was the first time she'd used my name, and the way she said it, with her usual note of impatience, but also a motherly sort of worry, had my belly clenching.

I startled as Ethan's hand slipped around my thigh beneath the water and he planted a swift kiss just above my pelvic bone before he vanished and I caught the darkened outline of him swimming deeper into the cave where Estelle wouldn't see him if he surfaced.

"Let's not keep him waiting," she prodded, holding out a towel for me as I waded to the edge and climbed up onto my feet and took it. "Can I at least go back to my room and change first?"

"Where are your clothes?"

I pursed my lips and glanced back to the water.

Estelle sighed, exasperated, and threw her hands up. "Then you'll go as you are. Don't want to keep him waiting, do we?"

Well, she clearly didn't. I really couldn't care less.

But truth be told I didn't want Estelle punished because *I* didn't care to follow orders.

I glanced back to see Ethan poking his head above water through the mist, a worried crook to his left brow. I tossed him a shrug that I hoped relayed to him I wasn't worried about this little impromptu meeting with my captor.

I didn't think it set his mind at ease, but I hoped it would quell him enough so he wouldn't attempt to follow me.

As we made our way through the torch-lit corridors, I shivered as the air became increasingly colder. My skin was still flushed from the spring and that only made the chill seem worse. The cold was burrowing into muscle and my teeth chattered. Soon it would be bone deep.

"That'll teach you to undress before you go jumping into the bath all willy nilly," Estelle chided, and I snorted through the shivers.

When we veered off to the right past the three-way fork, I stopped. "Estelle, where are you taking me?"

She paused and sighed, and I caught how her face fell in the flicker of firelight further down the corridor. Going left at the fork took us to the lab. And going straight led back to my chamber. I'd never gone right before.

"To the master's bedchamber."

My jaw twitched.

"Why?"

"Mind your head," was her only reply as she set off into the dark. "The ceiling dips low ahead."

Clenching my jaw, I hurried to follow her, my feet scratching against some sharp, loose stones. I winced as one sliced into my heel, drawing blood.

The darkness ahead abated in stages until I could discern a circular glow of orange light where the corridor ended and a bright, wide space began.

I quieted the beating of my heart and lifted my chin, checking quickly to ensure my towel was secure around me.

"Master," Estelle said, bowing as she reached the entrance to his chambers. "Shall I wait for her in the hall, sir?"

Azrael's voice boomed in the cave, "That won't

be necessary, Estelle. You may retire for the evening."

Estelle stiffened. She looked like she might be about to protest, but instead she quickly turned, tucked tail and rushed past me back the way we came. She didn't spare me even a cursory glance before she vanished.

"Are you going to come in? Or shall I come and retrieve you?"

With a chortle at the jibe, I strode into the chamber, refusing to be afraid.

Azrael and I had spent a lot of time together this past week. He was menacing as ever and infuriating to no end. But we'd formed a sort of forced camaraderie. Call it Stockholm syndrome or whatever you want, but even knowing he could kill me in the blink of an eye or compel me to lose my mind in a single glance, I didn't think he would ever actually do it.

It was either naivety or a brazen lack of respect for my own life, either way, he didn't phase me as much as he once did. Even if this little unplanned meeting had me second guessing him.

"Master," I said in a mocking tone with an exaggerated bow.

He smirked.

His chamber wasn't what I would've expected. Triple the size of mine, but almost barren. All it contained was a four-post bed at the center of the space with swatch of fabric hung between each post and enough pillows to suffocate several people at once. There was a roaring fire in a hearth to my left and threadbare rugs scattered about that helped keep the chill of the stone at bay. I inched closer to the fire, eager to warm my frozen bones.

"What is it you want?" I asked as I planted myself three feet in front of the flames, my body shaking as the warmth did its work to loosen all the tight muscle.

Azrael cocked his head at me, studying me. It made my insides twist. He sat on the edge of his bed, his hair loose around his severe face. His wide shoulders and thick neck didn't look as prominent in the black long-sleeve shirt he was wearing with the sleeves rolled to his elbows. His mismatched eyes glimmered in the firelight as a muscle in his jaw twitched.

"It's not what I want," he said finally. "It's what I'm prepared to give you."

I stilled at that, wondering what he was talking about. My mind ran through several scenarios.

Maybe he got me the new truck already?

Or he was letting me go?

Or…maybe he just wanted to give me a quick death?

That was a sort of gift, wasn't it? I hadn't given it to my prey often, and when I did, I hoped they were thankful for it.

Azrael chuckled and the sound rolled over me like a wool blanket. Rough, but also warm and comforting. His face looked so different when he smiled. Not like the monster I knew him to be, but like a man who had seen too much pain in his many years and could somehow still find it in his bent and battered heart to laugh.

I shook my head, my scowl returning. "What's so funny?"

"Oh, my dear Rose," he said between chuckles, rising from his bed to come to me by the fire. I tried not to move as his tall frame towered over me and he ran a thumb over my jaw. "Don't you think if I were going to kill you, I'd have done it already?"

Surprisingly, his words were vaguely reassuring. I batted his hand away from my face and had the satisfaction of watching him stiffen momentarily before he stepped away, something in his eyes changing. "Why did you summon me?" I tried again, my voice hardening.

Azrael gazed into the fire, resting his forearm on the top ledge of the hearth as he leaned in. The fire made his blue eye glimmer with flecks of gold and silver and his brown eye darken, flashing with flecks of red in the near-black iris.

Ocean shore and erupting volcano, my mind supplied. That's what his eyes looked like. *Dr. Jekyll and Mr. Hyde,* I mused, remembering how one second he could be perfectly calm and at ease, and the next he could let a glimpse of his true self—the monster lurking deep within—escape. I'd seen it once or twice now.

The first time in the spring only a day after I arrived.

And again, when he compelled all of my guys so they would never know how to find me.

Azrael bowed his head and grimaced. The light and shadows played on the planes of his pale face, making it look as though he could be carved from the stone he was leaning against. "I'm going to allow you to return to your…well, whatever they are to you. Your *friends*."

My heart soared and I could barely contain how it pounded with longing. *This better not be a fucking joke*, I thought to myself. If he was teasing me, I'd fucking cut him.

I'd been asking when we could go back every day since the day after we arrived back at the cave and his answer was always the same, *when I say so*.

"What changed?"

Azrael didn't move his gaze from the fire as he answered. "It doesn't matter."

My brows raised, but then I relaxed. He was right. What did I care what made him change his mind? But by the way his whole face was tense, and his lips pressed into a firm line, I knew he wasn't happy about this.

But for whatever reason, he was going to allow it, anyway.

"Thank you," I said, surprising myself and really meaning it. A part of myself cursed and shouted inside my mind, *you stupid bitch, why the hell are you thanking him? Are you mad? Have you gone soft?*

I cleared my throat and gave my head a slight shake, told myself to play nice.

Azrael tipped his head to the side, his gaze roamed over my face with something akin to pain in his eyes. Then it was gone, and the tepid mask of the great and terrible Azrael returned. He straightened. "I won't be escorting you this time. I will compel you both to sleep for the duration of the trip and to awaken once you've arrived."

My jaw clenched, but I nodded.

"Once you arrive, you will enter the apartment and you *will not leave* until I come to retrieve you. That part is not up for debate. Understood?"

I opened my mouth to protest. How could I stay in the apartment the *entire* time? Staying in this cave was making me stir-crazy and claustrophobic enough. I wanted to feel the moonlight on my face and breathe in the crisp air you could only find just before the dawn.

"You can agree, or you can remain here," Azrael spoke before I could retort. "I'm having a friend of mine put a warding spell around the building. She'll be finished by the time you get there. So long as you remain inside those walls, Raphael will not be able to find you."

"A *what* spell?"

"A warding spell."

"You know a witch?" I asked, an eyebrow raised. "I thought it was illegal for witches to share their magic with the other races?"

Azrael's full lips tugged up into a playful smirk. "It is. But for the right price, almost any allegiance can be bought."

I scowled.

"Anything else?" I asked him, my voice showing just how exasperated and exhausted I truly was beneath my carefully constructed veneer of alert calm.

His eyes lifted as he pondered the question. His bottom lip pursed. "No," he replied finally. "That's all. I'll return to collect you Sunday evening."

"What day is it today?" I asked, having absolutely no idea. I lost track sometime before we had even left to see the guys the first time around.

Azrael looked at me as though I'd grown another head. Like I should somehow be able to tell the passage of time, even entombed in stone that let in no natural light whatsoever. "It's Friday."

So, he was giving me two days…

It wasn't nearly enough, but I wasn't about to complain. Frost and Blake would be frantic with worry by now. If he'd have offered a mere hour, I'd have taken it. Two days was more than I dared hope for.

I was tempted to thank him again, but the more rational part of my brain shouted, *oh no you don't!*

Azrael lifted his arms and I wasn't sure what his aim was. My body reflexively began to move into a fighting stance, legs spread wide, but he only curled his hands around my upper arms. The skin of his palms was cool against my fire-flushed flesh and I shivered, resisting the urge to shake his hands off of me.

His gaze bored into me, his long hair falling forward to cover part of his right eye so I could only see the blue one. The ocean one. The Dr. Jekyll one. He was much less frightening with only that eye visible.

It looked like he was going to say something, but he was having trouble getting the words out. The silence became strained and awkward. I cringed inwardly.

Finally, Azrael sighed and let go of my arms. I breathed.

"I wanted to thank you, too," he whispered, unable to meet my eyes. "Even if we don't find what we hope to…I—well, I appreciate your willingness to cooperate."

A single, gruff laugh rose in my throat, but I quashed it. I couldn't smother the finger of fury zipping down my spine, though. Or how my chest tightened, and my gaze narrowed. "You didn't give me any choice," I reminded him with clenched fists.

His head snapped up and his eyes met mine once more.

Why couldn't he understand? I would have done anything to help my guys. To undo what they did to themselves. I would have eventually agreed to cooperate with Azrael if only to prove to both of us that what he wanted to accomplish was impossible. So I could sleep at night knowing I tried—*for them.*

I would have done as he asked *on my own terms.*

Azrael didn't give me that opportunity, though. He threatened me. He used my love for my guys against me. He made it so I had no other choice but to cooperate or I would see them hurt or worse…killed.

"You obviously haven't ever loved another person in your entire miserable life," I snapped, the logical part of my brain finally winning out over the weaker half—the half that was stupid enough to think that maybe Azrael wasn't all that bad.

Azrael's eyes darkened.

"If you had, you never would have used them against me. Only a monster would do that."

I was seething once I was finished, ready for a fight. I needed a punching bag, a training dummy, *something.*

It'd been too long since I let my fury out. I'd spent too long being a good little Rose. I could feel the pressure building in my chest. An image of Mom in a pool of blood flashed behind my eyelids and I winced.

I grit my teeth.

Why? Why did this always happen when I got worked up? If I didn't find an outlet for the anger soon it would come to a head, and I would be reduced to a puddle of tears on the cold stone floor. I wouldn't allow that. Not in front of *him*.

Physical pain was how I dealt with internal pain.

I stepped away from Azrael, breathing hard and low, in through my nose and out through my mouth.

There was murder in his gaze as he watched me trying to get control of myself. "There's a monster inside of you, too, Rose," he said in a deadpan voice. "Or are you too blind to recognize your own darkness for what it is?"

I hissed, my body coiling with the need to strike.

"It isn't *rage*," he said, and the malice in his eyes gave way. His face fell. "It's sorrow."

15

We woke up as the hearse came to a stop outside of the guys' apartment. Ethan rode in the back, asleep in the coffin, and Azrael mercifully allowed me to ride in the front with the driver. With me compelled to sleep for the entire trip he didn't see a reason why I should have to be locked in the death box with Ethan.

I'd scowled at him when he made the suggestion, wondering why the fuck he hadn't just done that the first time around.

It was near dawn when we arrived. Only about an hour out. As I came to and got my bearings, I noticed the sky was brightening near the horizon and I jumped out of the vehicle in a flash, practically tearing the back doors off the hearse in my haste to get Ethan up and out of the coffin.

The driver stood sentinel outside the back of the

hearse as I worked, watching with a blank expression and dead eyes. The poor fucker had likely been compelled half to death. "Would you get the other side?" I snipped at him as I began undoing the silver handle locks along the side where I was standing.

He did as I requested and then stepped back as Ethan shoved the lid of the coffin off and took a long and deep breath, squinting as his eyes adjusted to the light. His honey brown eyes widened as they took in the horizon.

"I know," I said in answer to the worried crease in his forehead. "Let's get you inside."

Ethan gulped, and then nodded, climbing from the death box with a stretch of his back. He stepped out of the back of the hearse as two young girls made their way past us on the street. Ethan stiffened as they crossed paths with us.

I noticed then how one of them was helping the other along, with an arm around the injured girl's shoulder. They wore short skirts and high heels. And it seems one of them had taken a pretty good fall. Her left knee was badly skinned, her pantyhose completely destroyed and caked with layers of wet and dried blood.

I snapped my attention back to Ethan, ready to put him into a strangle hold and drag him into the apartment if that's what it took. My body was on fire with adrenaline, preparing to take him down.

But…his shoulders sagged and the dilation in

his pupils lessened. He wasn't holding his breath anymore, and the terror in his gaze melted away, its place taken by a note of confusion and awe.

He smiled, turning back to me, incredulous. "Frost was right," he said in a breath, still grinning ear to ear. "That fucker was right…"

It took me a moment to piece together what he was saying, but when I did, I gasped. "My blood…"

Ethan nodded, pulling me into him to plant a hard kiss on my lips. When he pulled away, there were stars in his eyes. "This changes things," he said, and I thought he might've been on the verge of tears.

I wondered when the last time was that he could safely go out in public without worrying he might attack someone and not be able to help it. I imagined being faced with fresh blood and being wholly able to restrain himself was liberating. Like one of the shackles chaining him to the beast within had snapped off.

I smiled back at him and swatted his behind. "Rose Ward, assassin, lab-rat, and vampire juice-box extraordinaire," I chuckled. "It has a ring to it."

Ethan's face fell. "I didn't mean to insinuate—"

"Oh, shut up," I interrupted playfully, tossing him a wink. "I'll be your juice-box anytime."

He shook his head and together we crossed the street. I looked for any sort of signs that a witch had been here earlier in the night. I wasn't really sure what I was looking for, though. Maybe some blood on the walls. Some weird symbols. A salt line? But I saw nothing out of the ordinary.

Before Ethan could even get his keys out, the door flung open and Frost was standing in the entry, huffing, his hair disheveled and his bright green eyes wide and wild. "Where the fuck have you been?"

"We—"

"It's been a week," he growled, glaring at us—scrutinizing each and every inch of me, and then every inch of Ethan. Searching for signs of harm.

Behind us, the hearse started to back up and drove off.

"Is he here?"

"No," I answered. "Just us."

His brows lowered. "Did you escape?"

I sighed. "No. He's given me forty-eight hours… then I have to go back."

Ethan's brow drew down, but he didn't comment. I realized a little belatedly that I'd said 'I' and not '*we*'. I had no intention of allowing him to return with me to the cave, but he didn't need to know that yet.

"Where's Blake?" Ethan asked, taking the words right out of my mouth.

Frost moved out of the way and ushered us inside. "Come on, get your asses inside. It's not safe to be out right now."

What?

"He's in the shower," Frost added, stomping up the stairs.

"What do you mean, it's not safe?" Ethan asked, lithely taking the stairs two at a time to keep up with Frost. From this vantage point I had a fucking fantastic view.

Frost was still tense as hell. I could see his hands clenched at his sides and when he turned to glare at Ethan, the thick vein popping out of his neck. "Because they're still looking for her," he all but spat at Ethan. "Or did you forget there's still a bounty on her head?"

I was taken aback. Ethan may not have forgotten, but I almost had. *Damn.* "Are they here? In Baton Rouge?"

Frost paused at the top of the stairs before opening the door. He breathed heavily and then with a determined look, shoved the door to the apartment open. "Yes," he said as he stepped inside. "But it's not just here. Blake and I have been keeping an eye on things and an ear to the ground. Word has spread, and the bounty on your head has doubled. Raphael is growing restless and he won't stop until he finds you."

Frost's face was beet-red when he finally turned back to face us as Ethan closed the door. My chest squeezed at the pain I found hiding behind the hardness in his gaze. "I'm not even sure you should be here," he said begrudgingly. "I'm not sure it's safe…at least—" he stopped himself, gritting his teeth. "At least wherever Azrael has you, they won't be able to find you."

I knew it was killing him to admit that. That he —that *they*—were not enough to protect me from so many foes. "It's alright," I told him, shrugging. "Azrael had a witch put a ward up around this building. As long as I stay inside it, I can't be tracked here."

Frost frowned. "A witch was here?"

"Azrael employs a witch?" Ethan asked, and I realized I hadn't told him, either.

I nodded. "Yeah. So dislodge the stick from your ass," I told Frost with a cheeky grin and a wink, trying to lighten the mood. "I'll be just fine so long as I stay inside."

Frost strode past me and threw the deadbolt on the door home, effectively locking us all inside. I shuddered involuntarily, a little meek voice in the back of my mind wondered when, *or if,* I would ever be truly free again…

I shook my head and shut up. "Come here, big guy," I said with the best smile I could conjure, opening my arms.

The corner of Frost's lips pulled up and he shook his head at me. I'm not sure what I expected, but I yelped as he lifted me from the floor with a strong arm under my butt and the other wrapped tightly across my back. I buried myself in the crook of his neck, taking a deep breath of worn leather and tangy aftershave. I sighed.

"I missed you," I whispered, my heart aching at the tenderness in the way he held me.

He planted a kiss in my hair, and I felt some of the tension leave his shoulders. "I missed you, too, Rosie."

16

The shower was still running as I crept down the hallway. Frost and Ethan warned that I should wait until he came out, but I didn't want to wait. I'd waited long enough to see them. A week apart felt like a goddamned year and I wouldn't wait another second. Not when I had another choice.

Plus, I wasn't about to pass up the chance to see a dripping wet and naked Blake. His glorious body wrapped in coiling black tattoos. His near-black hair shining and damp. My inner lioness was already roaring and ready to pounce. The sexy little minx in my mind purring as I quietly turned the slot in the lock with my thumbnail.

"Frost, you need something?" Blake hollered from inside, and I heard the water shut off.

Damn. I hadn't been quiet enough.

"It's not Frost," I said as I nudged the door open and was met with a wall of warm steam and the scents of vanilla and suede.

"Rose..." Blake breathed as the door clicked shut behind me.

His dark eyes widened as they took me in.

My own widened in response, drawing a line down his chiseled chest and abs, and lower to his half-hard cock, and the thick muscle of his thighs. I admired the way his tattoos wrapped around his biceps and ran down his forearms. How they crawled over his hard pecks and up the sides of his neck. The start of another tattoo began on his left side and followed the curve of his inner groin to wrap around his right thigh.

I gulped.

He was a fucking masterpiece.

"Rose," Blake said again, louder this time as he almost tripped out of the shower in his haste to get to me. His hands lifted to cup my face, his fingers warm and wet. He searched my eyes, as though he was afraid this was a mere dream and we would wake up any second.

"I'm here," I told him, laying a hand against his hand still cupping my cheek. I smirked. "I told you guys—you're all fucking stuck with—"

He kissed me. His lips crashed against mine, and his warmth seeped into me as warm droplets shook loose from his hair and scattered like rain down my cheeks. He pulled away too soon, and I moved to wrap my arms around him.

His spine went rigid as my hand met the skin of his back. He sucked in a breath and pushed my hand away, stepping back to put three feet of space between us.

The wonder was gone from his features. His gray eyes had darkened to a shade closer to black. The muscles in his face were taut and drawn as he stared at the floor.

"I'm sorry, I didn't—"

"No," he all but growled, his chest rising and falling faster than it was a moment before.

I stepped closer, and he stepped back again. "Blake? What is it?"

He swallowed. "Just…" he started, his tone hard and icy. "Just get out."

He might as well have driven an icepick into my chest. *What?* "But I—"

"*Please*," he ground out, backing up until he was able to grab a towel from the hook next to the shower.

With my mind racing and not another word out of my mouth, I turned and left the room. I hadn't missed how he reacted when I touched him. Or how he never once turned his back to me. My stomach soured as my mind conjured all sorts of horrible things he could have been hiding.

What happened to him?

We all knew Blake's father was a total fucking loser. The worst sort of asshole. A memory flickered at the edges of my mind. Of a time when I'd jumped on Blake's back when we were kids. I'd only meant to be playful. I was just trying to surprise him.

And he'd thrown me off as though I was on fire. I'd hit the ground hard and banged my head. He'd had to carry me to the nurse's station in the school, the whole time apologizing profusely. Near the point of tears in his guilt for hurting me.

I'd never done that again. By the following year everyone knew better than to sneak up on Blake. Everyone knew he didn't like to be touched. But I always thought it was just *other* people he didn't like touching him. People he didn't know. He used to let *me* hug him. Let *me* run my fingers through his hair. Held my hand when we ran from Frost after dumping a gallon of cold water on his head the morning after the last day of school. I was the exception, wasn't I?

Me and the guys?

As I shut the door behind me, my legs wobbled, and my heart grew heavy as I realized I wasn't really a part of their *whole* anymore. Hadn't been for a long time. And where I'd accepted them back into my heart almost from the first moment I'd seen them, regardless of whether they'd become the things I hunted, they may not have accepted me back into the fold so easily.

At least, it seemed, Blake hadn't.

I steeled myself, and forced the thoughts from my mind, stalking back towards the living area. *That's alright*, I told myself. *It's fine.*

"Frost," I called, halfway down the hall now. "Got anything to eat in this place? I'd kill for some Cheetos and a slushie."

An hour later, I had a convenience store feast. Cheetos and a Sprite slushie along with a cup of five-cent candies, three chocolate bars, a bag of peppered jerky, and a case of Gatorade. I could smell the nutty aroma of cheap coffee percolating in the kitchen. It was so beautiful.

"I fucking love you guys," I told them as I inhaled half the bag of Cheetos, sucking the orange powder from my fingertips.

Even though I was fed well in the cave—every meal seemed to be meticulously crafted to include each food group and the perfect portion sizes—I never had what I was really craving…food that *doesn't* exactly fit in with any identifiable food group.

I started feeling more myself after the first brain freeze from my slushie subsided. Any traces of soreness or aches I'd been carrying since my last visit to the lab evaporated.

"Better?" Ethan asked with an eyebrow raised and a smirk pulling at one corner of his lips.

"Much," I replied, polishing off the slushie with a wink in his direction.

He chuckled.

"So," I began, setting down my empty cup and brushing the orange crumbs from my shirt. "The fuckers are in Baton Rouge now? Do you think they tracked me somehow?"

Frost crossed his burly arms over his chest and grimaced. "Nah. I think they tracked *us*, but I can't be sure. The city was crawling with vamps before you were captured by Azrael, it's possible someone could've seen us with you and tracked us back to Baton Rouge."

"Can they find you here?"

"Let 'em try," Blake said, pulling my focus to where he was coming down the hallway, his hair still damp, but now he was fully clothed. His gaze swept over me and I watched his adams apple bob in his throat before he sat down in the armchair across from the couch.

Frost leaned forward and I turned my attention back to him. "We've been taking them out one by one," he admitted, gritting his teeth.

"Eight in the last week," Blake added.

"You've been doing *what*?" My brows raised and my heart thudded against my ribcage.

Frost cocked his head at me. "What? Should

we've just kept letting them multiply, so the city was overrun with them by the time you returned?"

I frowned. "It's dangerous, Frost," I all but growled, completely losing my appetite. "What if Raphael was out there, hmm?"

Blake scoffed. "As if that bastard would do any of his own dirty wor—"

"Or any vampire over the age of fifty," I spat, cutting him off.

"You underestimate us," Blake said, deadpan, his black eyes glittering with fury.

Ha!

"We hunt vampires, Rosie," Frost said, leaning back in his armchair with a sigh. "Just like you did. And we're damn good at it."

I shook my head, my eyes casting a wide arc over the ceiling. I resisted the urge to groan. I remembered when Frost told me that they changed themselves to fight back against the creatures of the night. To find their way back to me. He'd said they hunt the ones who deserve it.

I'd been so furious and shaken at the time I hadn't really put much thought into it, but now… now I was imagining all sorts of scenarios where they could get themselves seriously hurt. Even killed.

All it would take is a second. A split second. A single wrong move.

"It's no more dangerous for us as it is for you,"

Ethan chimed in, the voice of reason. "I understand your worry, but it's misplaced."

I ground my teeth and tried to shove the thoughts from my mind. He was right, as usual. They fought together. Three young vamps against one older one was an even match. It really wasn't much different than what I did.

Did.

I hated that it was suddenly past tense.

I'm a vampire hunter. It's what I do.

Without that, what am I?

Just…Rose?

I had no other skills. I didn't go to college or university. I would never be a mother—I'd decided that a long time ago—I wouldn't wish this existence on anyone, least of all a future daughter. So, what was left?

Would I ever be able to go back to hunting? Or would I be relegated to being *hunted* for the rest of my life, instead? I doubted Raphael would ever give up. Someone a thousand-or-so-years-old would be well-versed in the art of patience.

"What's wrong?" Ethan asked after the silence stretched on for a few more minutes.

I shook my head, dislodging the disquieting thoughts, and cleared my throat. I looked up with a half-hearted grin. "Nothing."

I glanced around at Frost, Blake, and Ethan, and realized that I didn't have any reason to be disappointed. I had *them.* I didn't think I would ever have them again, but here they were. And when Azrael was finished with me, maybe we could go someplace together. Somewhere far away from here, where Raphael couldn't find us. I'd hardly touched a penny of the inheritance from my mother, though it wasn't much. And then there was the house—I could sell it.

I'd trade hunting for the three of them any day. Besides, maybe they needed a few vampire exterminators in Tanzania, or maybe Timbuktu…

This time, my smile was real.

We'd figure this shit out one way or another. Together.

I tore open the bag of jerky and willed my muscles to relax as I sank back into the sofa. "So," I said, popping a chunk of peppered beef in my mouth. "What has everyone been up to for the last ten or so years?"

Frost snorted.

Ethan's cheeks dimpled with a tense grin.

Blake looked away—a darkness shrouding his already dark eyes.

"Ok then, I'll start…"

We sat like that for hours. Me, stuffing my face with junk food and Gatorade. Them, answering my hail of questions. My story was simple. I'd been institutionalized. Then thrown in foster care. I had several shitty fosters, including but not limited to;

one pedophilic drunk fucker who had a thing for feet, a woman who locked me in my 'room' for days at a time, and a couple who treated me as though I were a feral animal in need of caging—they may not have been wrong.

Then my power to compel got stronger. *I* got stronger. And I decided I didn't need to be a mouse in the trap anymore. I'd been living alone since I was sixteen. Started training before my seventeenth birthday. Killed my first vamp before my eighteenth.

Been doing it ever since.

I glazed over the darker bits for the guys, not wanting them to feel any remorse or guilt for any of it since it truly wasn't their fault. If anything, I had them to thank for getting me through it all. It was their faces—their memory—that kept me from succumbing to the dark.

"And then she took off," Frost said. "She calls about twice a year, but I stopped picking up a while back."

His mother had always been a real piece of work. She'd had four marriages under her belt by the time I was taken away, and it seemed she wasn't finished. Frost told me he watched two more husbands come and go before the most recent one convinced her to pack up and move to Rome with him. She hadn't been back to visit. Not even once since she left six years before.

My face fell. "I'm sorry."

Frost's face hardened. "Don't be," he told me. "I'm not."

I got up and walked over to him to plop myself down in his lap. He tugged me to him with a grin and squeezed my ribs, trying to play off his emotions. At least he didn't have to worry about hiding what he was from her. That could get tricky.

"What about your family, Ethan?"

Ethan had a sad smile as he asked me, "What family?"

I cocked my head at him.

What?

Ethan wasn't close with his relatives, but he had a lot of them. His parents were microbiologists and even though they had the biggest, nicest house on our block, they were never actually inside of it. Ethan spent all of his time alone in that big house while they flew from conference to conference—from university to university. And though he had about a million cousins and several aunts and uncles, because his parents were so closed off from them, so was he. He only saw them once every few years around the holidays.

"What do you mean?"

"I'm dead," he told me plainly, his steeped tea eyes tipping down at the corners. "Well, undead, I guess, but they didn't need to know that."

"You…you faked your own death?" I asked,

incredulous and trying to catch up to what he was telling me.

He nodded. "My heart doesn't beat. I don't have to breathe. It was easy to fake it for the authorities."

"Easy to compel the coroner that an autopsy wouldn't be necessary," Frost added.

"And then easy to dig him back out of his own grave after the funeral," Blake finished.

Ethan had essentially killed himself. I could hardly believe it. My chest ached for him. I knew he wasn't close with them, but his parents had cared for him in their own way. When they were home, his mother would cook amazing meals for them all, and his father would take him out hiking. They made sure he was taken care of.

They weren't like Frost's floozy, absentee mother who I would deck in the face if I ever saw her again, or like Blake's asshole father, who I would gladly send to an early grave if he hadn't found one already.

Ethan dropped his gaze. "I still check on them from time to time. The first year was hard for them, but they're doing fine now. Better than fine, actually."

I nodded, unsure what to say except, "And what about you?"

He managed a small half-grin. "I'm good."

I turned to Blake, about to ask him how his mother was. She'd been ill ten years ago before everything that happened and barely left the house. She spent most of her time in bed with the TV set to the game-show channel. But she was a nice enough woman from what I saw of her. We never hung out at Blake's house, though, so I didn't see her very much.

"What about—"

I caught a look from Ethan. His eyes met mine and he shook his head.

I looked from him to Blake. Blake still had his gaze fixed to the shaggy rug. His hands were curled tightly around the armrests of his chair.

It felt like I just swallowed a bucket of lead. *What happened to him?*

Later, Ethan mouthed to me and then got up to clear away the wrappers strewn over the coffee table.

The tension was tangible in the air as the silence stretched on. All the color was draining from Blake's face and I thought any second now he was going to burst. I scrambled to change the subject, rising to help Ethan clean up the mess I'd made. I supposed when all you consumed was blood, there was very little food mess.

"Show me your shop?" I asked Ethan as we made our way to the kitchen, eager to escape the heaviness in the room. "I want to see what you do."

Ethan smiled at me. "Yeah. We can go down the

back stairwell," he offered. "Technically you won't be leaving the building that way."

"Alright—"

"No." Blake's gruff voice sawed through the air like a serrated knife.

"Blake," Frost warned, his voice hard.

"No. She should know," he replied tersely, rising from the armchair with his spine ramrod straight. "Let's talk," he said, his gaze flickering to meet mine for the briefest of seconds. "In private."

I bit my lip, my blood chilling in my veins. "Ok."

He didn't pause as he strode down the hallway. He didn't turn back to see if I was following.

Ethan ran a hand down my arm, smoothing the goosebumps that'd risen there. "He doesn't like talking about it," he said in a low voice. "Be patient."

I nodded, wondering what the fuck I was about to find out.

Who was I going to have to kill?

His father's chilling stare flashed in a distant memory through my mind and I shuddered. There was always something about that man that didn't sit right with me. We all knew he was an asshole. He'd shouted profanities at a fourteen-year-old Blake right in their front yard once, in front of all the neighbors. Called him pathetic. Useless. A waste of skin.

We all hated him. He was an ass—there was no denying it.

Had he done something worse than verbal abuse? I'd seen enough of the world now to know there was far worse a person could do to another person.

I never told Blake, but that time out in the yard, after his father was through yelling, I saw him raise his hand. He didn't strike, but I was so afraid he would. So *furious.* I was the one who called the police that day. I was the reason Mr. Silvers was taken away in cuffs to sober up in the drunk tank overnight.

I prayed that a night behind bars would be enough to make him think twice about *ever* raising his hand against his son again. And it seemed for a while that it had. Mr. Silvers stopped shouting in the night. Blake seemed happier. His mother even seemed to take a turn for the better—going outside to tend to her wilting garden along the front of the house.

What if it hadn't been enough?

Somberly, I followed Blake to an open door at the end of the hall and to the left.

When I stepped inside, it was dark, the only light a softly glowing blue light beside the night-stand. "Close the door, Rose," Blake ordered, and I took the last step over the threshold, letting the door fall closed behind me.

17

The room was cloaked in a shadow and smelled faintly of suede and vanilla, as though a candle had been burning only moments before. There was another scent, too. A peculiar one. Like oiled rope and warm leather—not scents I was used to finding in a bedroom.

I could just make out Blake's outline, with his torso hunched over his knees he sat on the edge of a double bed covered in luxe black bedding. I went to him, careful to step around a strange contraption hanging from the ceiling. I thought maybe it was some sort of light fixture, but saw no bulbs hanging from it.

When I was in front of him, and he made no move to raise his head or to speak, I knelt, putting myself squarely in front of him, at eye-level between his knees. I didn't dare touch him. After the way he reacted in the bathroom to a simple embrace, I was afraid I might not ever be able to touch him again. Not if he was going to look at me in horror—as though caressed by the blade of a knife instead of the soft pads of my fingers.

"You don't have to talk to me if you don't want to," I told him in a whisper, my throat suddenly dry. "I can wait. I'll wait as long as you need me to, Blake. I—"

He moved his hands away from his face and I was floored at the sheer amount of pain radiating out from his eyes to coat me in a layer of icy dread that had me shivering against its chill.

I couldn't help myself, the words tumbled out of my lips before I could stuff them back in. "What happened to you?" My voice broke and I had to clench my hands into tight fists to keep myself from reaching out to console him.

My heart broke to see him in so much anguish.

He swallowed and his gaze dropped from mine to the floor again. His beautiful face was twisted in anguish he was clearly working so hard to hide. His body almost shaking from the effort of keeping it contained.

Then suddenly, as swiftly as it came, it went. The storm clouds in his eyes cleared and the storm raging beneath his flesh stilled. Quieted.

"I'm going to tell you everything," he said without feeling. "I'll say it once, and then never again."

"You don't have to—"

"I do. You're one of us. *Ours.*"

My chest swelled and my throat grew thick.

Blake inhaled deeply, his chest expanding before he let loose a long, breathy sigh. "You deserve to know why I can't..." he paused, switching his train of thought. "You need to know what my triggers are. I don't want you to think my reactions are your fault. And I don't want to hurt you."

Hurt me?

"How—"

"Rose, just listen."

I zipped my lips.

I never did know when to shut up.

Rocking back on my heels, I moved to sit cross legged in front of him, staring up through his knees at his anguished face. I could only make out the planes of him in the dark. The sharp line of his jaw and cheekbones. The dark hollows of his eyes. The curling tattoos creeping like vines up his neck. He was wearing only a t-shirt now. His usual jacket discarded on the bed.

I clasped my fingers together tightly in my lap and listened, my body tense as though preparing for a physical assault. My muscles coiled to—*to strike or to run*, I wasn't sure. I only knew that I wasn't going to like whatever I was about to hear, and my body was rebelling—my ears ringing in the quiet as though they could block out what he was about to say.

"My mother died," he said after a time.

I opened my mouth to speak again, but he cut me a side-long glance and I closed it. *Dead?* She'd been sick for so long. I shouldn't have been surprised. But a part of me always thought she wasn't *actually sick*. Like maybe she just didn't have as much energy as most people and needed to lay down a lot. And then when I grew older and wiser, looking back I thought maybe she suffered from some form of depression. I still didn't know. By the time I returned to my hometown, Blake's house was no longer The Silvers'.

It belonged to another family. They'd painted the house yellow and the door bright cherry red. The shiny new mailbox at the end of the driveway wasn't the rusted out black box anymore, instead it was one of those fancy ones that looked like a miniature house.

I knew right away that the place didn't belong to them anymore.

"It was cancer," he explained.

"Undiagnosed," he then added with a note of gruff malice in his voice, wringing his hands in front of him. "When she got worse, I tried to get him to let me take her to the hospital, but he refused."

"Your father?"

He nodded. "He said she was fine. That we couldn't afford the medical bills and that she wasn't really sick anyway. He was—well, looking back now, I think he must've been in denial."

"When did she pass?"

"Less than a year after they took you away."

Tears pricked at my eyes, but I knew from the look in his that this wasn't even close to the worst part. Whatever he was going to tell me next was what I needed to be bracing for.

"He went fucking nuts, Rose."

No.

If that motherfucker hurt my Blake—

"He punished me for her passing. Blamed me. Told me she was never the same after she had me. That I was the cause of her sickness."

I clenched my jaw to keep myself in check. I coaxed the sleeping dragon in my belly back to laying and whispered to the darkness in my mind that we would get our vengeance in blood. Patience.

Patience.

"Blake, I'm—"

He hushed me sharply, grinding his teeth behind lips pressed into a tight line. "He…he started to make good on his promises after she was gone."

I knew those promises. Or at least some of them. If you were within twenty feet of the Silver's residence any time after nine in the evening, you'd have heard them, too.

I should cut you for saying that!

You're lucky I don't put this out on your face!

You ever talk back to me again and I'll put you in a pine box!

They were idle threats.

Weren't they?

Blake reached out a shaking hand and tugged my hand from my lap. He unfurled my clenched knuckles and I swallowed. He held my hand tightly, palm out. So tightly it almost hurt. With his other hand, he lifted his shirt and guided my hand around his side to his back. He hesitated before placing my palm flat against his skin.

My calloused palm met raised tissue. A ridgeline of it. I almost gagged as my stomach turned and acidic bile rose in my throat. Blake held onto my wrist, not allowing me to explore more than the reach of my fingertips. All the while clenching and unclenching his jaw. Hard breaths flaring his nostrils.

The ridge of scar tissue was long. A jagged line. Not unlike the scar on his chest—or the one across my neck. Below that line, were three other scars. Circular ones. The skin puckered and uneven. *Burn scars,* I realized with a jolt that made my hairs stand on end.

Hot tears welled in my eyes and spilled over as I strained to feel more of his back. The further I reached, the more scars I found. His entire back was a roadmap of scar tissue. A morbid patchwork of pain.

Oh god…

His grip tightened on my wrist and then he pulled my hand away. "That's enough," he snapped, his breaths evening back out the instant I moved my hand away.

My heart ached for him. Guilt gripped me from the inside, like fists around my lungs. It was hard to breathe.

What had his father *done* to him? For how long?

"I'm—" I began, trying to keep the strain from my voice. "I'm so sorry I wasn't…"

"It's not your fau—"

"I should've done something. If I thought he would actually—"

"Rose—"

The tears began to dry, and a hot and sizzling fury flooded my veins. "He'll pay for this," I hissed, shaking now, getting ready to stand. Azrael's orders be damned. I could be back in Silverton within a day or two if I drove without stopping. I could have Mr. Silvers begging for death within forty-eight hours. I'd draw it out. I'd cut him. I'd burn him.

And then I'd fucking chop off his junk and stuff it down his throat until he choked on it.

I couldn't remember the last time I was this murderous. My teeth ground together as my mind whirred.

Blake's hand snaked out and snatched me by the wrist, stopping me. "Rose." Blake's voice was hard.

"You can't stop me," I warned. People like Mr. Silvers didn't deserve forgiveness. They deserved pain and suffering and an eternity in hell.

"I wouldn't," Blake said, releasing me. He looked up into my amber eyes and I read the meaning hiding in his deadly gaze. "If he weren't already dead."

I frowned, and then it dawned on me. "How?" I asked, though I thought I already knew.

"Ethan and Frost found out what was going on."

Again, my heart ached that I wasn't there for him. To stop the monster he called father from torturing him. It *hurt* more than words could express. But at least he had Ethan and Frost…

At least he wasn't alone.

"I told them I didn't want the police involved, so they came over and threatened him. Ethan said he had footage of what my father did to me and would plaster it on the news and use it to make sure he got life in prison. Frost told him he would set the house on fire with him inside it and make sure he couldn't get out—make it look like an accident."

Blake laughed a bit at that. "I felt so weak, Rose. I knew he was in pain and I just kept expecting him to stop. To change. To see what he was doing to me and realize he was sick, too."

Unconsciously, I reached out to caress his face. He flinched a little, but when I went to remove my hand, he held it against his cheek, instead.

"Anyway," Blake said, twining his fingers with mine as he drew my hand away. "Suffice it to say my father didn't like being threatened." The low tone of his voice skittered down my spine and I shivered.

"What did he do?" I breathed, grasping his hand tighter.

"He tried to make good on the one promise he hadn't yet…"

I'll put you in a pine box…

Blake shook his head. "He might've succeeded if the guys hadn't been watching and listening. They came in and found me…" he paused, and I couldn't take seeing the shame cross his dark eyes.

He had *nothing* to be ashamed of. Didn't he see that?

A father was supposed to be someone you could trust. Someone you could count on to *protect* you. Prescott Silvers was no father. He was the fucking devil incarnate.

"They found me half dead in the living room. Dad was in the bedroom, putting the combination into the safe where he kept his pistol."

I winced, bracing myself for what he would say next.

"He managed to get a shot off before they managed to disarm him. He was aiming for me, but Ethan took the hit—the idiot."

My golden knight. I wasn't surprised. Not in the least.

"He got Ethan in the stomach. I thought he was going to die…"

I could only imagine the horror of that moment. I knelt back down to see into Blake's eyes, still clutching his hand in mine, urging him to go on.

"Frost had him in a headlock. His gun was only a few feet away from me on the carpet."

I knew what would happen next.

Blake may not have stood up for himself. He may not have been willing to fight his own father *for himself.* But for Frost and Ethan…

It wasn't a question.

"Frost saw me grab the gun and shoved my father away a split second before I put a bullet between his eyes."

"You did the right thing," I told him, imploring him to see that.

His face was hard as he nodded. "I told myself that for a long time. I was only sixteen when it happened. They sent me to juvie. I was there until I turned eighteen. Ethan and Frost were there to pick me up the day I got out. We've been together ever since."

We sat quietly for a moment as his words sunk in.

I rubbed my thumb over the back of his hand. I could tell he was finished talking. He'd said he would tell me what happened once and then never again. Though I had more questions, I refrained from asking them. Not wanting him to feel forced to share more than he had already. I would ask the other guys later. I wouldn't make Blake talk about it anymore.

"So now you know," Blake sighed. "It's why I can't handle being touched."

"I understand. And I'm sorry."

"You didn't know."

"This," I said, rubbing my thumb over the back of his hand again. "This seems to be okay."

He nodded solemnly. "It's my back mostly," Blake explained. "The bastard liked to put his marks where no one would be able to see them."

I grit my teeth.

"It's better than it was before. *Any* touch set me off for years. It wasn't until we turned that I got some of myself back."

I offered him a pained smile.

Where the change had affected Ethan with disgust in himself—with hopelessness—it had strengthened Blake. I could see it now. How immortality had re-birthed him into a stronger, more confident version of himself. I was suddenly so glad he'd made the choice to do it. If only for that reason.

If only to attain a modicum of peace and acceptance of the events that shaped him.

"Stop looking at me like that," Blake said suddenly, taking me aback. He released my hand and I stiffened. "Don't look at me like I'm broken. I resent that."

I schooled my features and gave him a single terse nod. I knew the look he was talking about. It was the same one the doctors and police officers and psychologists gave me once upon a time. I hated that look, too.

"You're the strongest of us," I whispered. "Always have been. If anything, what you've just told me proves that."

He looked at me doubtfully, but I was entirely sincere.

Once he saw that, some of the chill left his gaze. After a moment, a little bit of some other emotion crossed his handsome face. A flicker of fire in his eyes. The slight twist of his lips.

I cocked my head at him, confused as his fiery gaze roved over my body. "That's enough depressing shit for one day, don't you think?"

My brows drew together. *What was he playing at?*

He reached over and tapped the softly glowing blue light on the nightstand—making it glow a bit brighter, illuminating the space around us. I took a cursory glance around and froze.

The *lights* I thought I'd walked into earlier weren't lights at all. They were a bunch of loosely tied ropes hanging from thick metal anchors in the ceiling. And across the room, there was a sort of den that stretched around the edge of the long wall.

I could only make out part of what was inside, but I saw polished black leather and deep crimson velvet. The edge of a rack with leather manacles at the top and bottom. The back end of a rather oddly shaped chair *thing*. A mirror set in the mouth of the den area showed me a reflection of more items deeper within, though I couldn't entirely make them out.

I thought I saw a sex swing hanging from the ceiling. And along the back wall of the space—an array of colorful looking bits and bobs. Some I recognized, and others I didn't. It was quite the collection of…*toys*.

Oh my.

Immediately, my breaths came heavier, and an ache spread low in my belly, making my thighs squeeze together and a swelling heat fog my mind.

I glanced back to Blake, mouth agape. I knew he was still hurting, but it was clear he was trying to change the subject. To take his mind off of it. And since I was the reason he'd had to reopen those long-scabbed-over wounds. I supposed it was sort of my duty to help him forget again. If only for a little while.

"Since I have you here," Blake purred, reaching out a hand to me. I took it and stood with him, my stomach dropping. His gaze flicked to the rope contraption hanging from the ceiling and back to me. "Do you trust me?"

18

"I trust you," I told him, but I was a little thrown off. "You want to do this *now*?"

Nervous flutters swirled around in my belly, waking the slumbering dragon and the little minx.

"Why wait?"

I shut my mouth. Suddenly unable to think of a single reason why we shouldn't. The darkness and pain of only moments before shrunk back into the corners as Blake beamed at me—the light of his grin bright enough to chase even the darkest shadows away. Why did he have to be so infuriatingly perfect? How could I say no to that face?

Not that I wanted to say no.

Why the hell would I want to do that?

I'd have to be insane to refuse him. I'd been dreaming about him since I missed my chance to have him the last time I'd seen them. I'd been vividly imagining all the erotic scenarios and naked escapades we could get into together.

"Alright," I said in a coy voice, pulling my bottom lip between my teeth to stifle a premature moan.

I let him lead me over to the ropes hanging from the ceiling and he let go of my hand, beginning to deftly untie the loose knots keeping them from reaching the floor. The ropes unfurled one by one until there were at least ten sections, each probably close to thirty feet in length hanging from the ceiling to pool in little spirals of russet gold on the carpet.

"These are made from conditioned hemp," he said, running his fingers over a length of rope. "Here, feel them."

I swallowed hard before walking forward to take a bit of rope in my fingers. It was soft, with just the right amount of softness. I bit my lips again. "And what exactly are we going to do with them?"

I couldn't help the blush that rose to my cheeks. I was clueless when it came to this sort of thing. Like any normal person, I enjoyed a good fucking, but Mr. Dickins was the only trustworthy *man* I'd had in…well, since forever.

Rose Ward didn't get close to people.

Ha! I certainly didn't trust any other human being enough to allow them to blindfold me or bind my hands. But Blake and the guys weren't just any other humans.

They were *mine.*

And not humans at all. Not anymore.

He'd asked me if I trusted him, and the answer was *yes*.

Always.

"You don't have to do anything," he replied with a note of excitement in his tone. "In fact, I don't want you to move at all."

I stopped breathing as he stepped closer, a blue glimmer in his eyes from the dim light on the nightstand. I shuddered as his hands ran down my arms.

"Will it hurt?" I managed.

He stopped his soft touches and touched a knuckle to the hollow beneath my chin to tip my head up to look him in the eyes. "No," he said simply. "This isn't about pain. I would never hurt you, Rose."

The ropes dangling behind him begged to differ. What would he do with them, then?

"This is about pleasure. About…*beauty*. And you'll be my most exquisite masterpiece."

Blake moved my hair from my breasts, laying it behind my shoulders so he could unzip my top. The air in the room was warm, but the second it hit my breasts, they hardened, and my core tightened.

"It's called Shibari," he explained as he undressed me with practiced restraint. "I'm going to tie you up."

Oh fuck…

"And then I'm going to suspend you from the ceiling…"

Warmth pooled between my thighs as he coaxed my pants and panties down to my ankles, his breath brushing against my pussy as he helped me step out of the pool of clothing.

"…and then I'm going to fuck you until you cum…again…and again…*and again…*"

He stood; his obsidian eyes boring into me. He licked his lips and I fought the urge to touch him, already shaking with a combination of unchecked desire and restlessness. "Do I have your consent?"

I didn't hesitate before responding this time. I wanted this. I wanted him. I wanted to know every facet of him. What made him tick. What turned him on. All of it. The good, the bad, the ugly, and the bizarre. Every. Fucking. Bit. "You have all of me."

He smiled. "Good."

Blake took me gently by the elbows and moved me into the center of the ropes. Wordlessly, he tapped something on his phone and then tossed the device onto the bed. Music drifted out from some unseen speakers, surrounding us in a hauntingly beautiful melody. Lyrics sung in an ethereal voice, in a different language, caressed my ears, mixing with the drumbeats and cello in a way that made me sigh and shiver all at once.

"It's beautiful," I said.

"No talking," Blake replied gruffly, and I saw the depth of his own desire etched into his stone carved features. His eyes darkened and I saw the beginnings of his fangs as he tugged my arms behind me and locked my arms together, coaxing me to wrap my hands around my forearms near my elbows.

The ropes slid over my wrists with little *shhh* noises as he wrapped and tied and knotted. Around my wrists and then across my back and around to my front, above my breasts and across my chest. The sensation of the rope tightening over me had my body screaming for release. By the time he had my entire torso and arms finished, I couldn't move more than half an inch.

I moaned as he set to work between my legs, knotting rope along my thighs and calves until they were pulled up from the ground, my legs bound into bent angles, spread wide.

He was right. This was *art.* And the artist worked with a furrowed, sweat dampened brow and a determined look in his eyes. No knot was insignificant. No movement unmeasured. He was precise.

And when my body was finally fully suspended, he rocked back on his heels to look at me.

He'd pulled on the ropes to bring me higher from the floor and adjusted the lengths until I was suspended with my body upright. The ropes around my chest and across my back were attached to others that supported me like a cradle, allowing me to lean a little backward. Enough so that the angle of my pussy was perfectly aligned to a level where his cock could glide in unobstructed.

Surprisingly, he'd been right. It didn't hurt. There were so many lengths of rope supporting me in so many different places, that no one place felt strained. The balance of my weight was equally distributed in a way that only caused lines of pressure across my body. And…I kind of liked it.

It wasn't pain, but close enough to that invisible line so it could be called extreme pleasure.

Blake's dark eyes traveled over me with a keen and unscrupulous gleam. It should be illegal for anyone to look as incredible sexy as he did marveling his work.

"You're the most beautiful thing I've ever seen," he said with reverence, and his adams apple bobbed with a hard gulp as he righted himself. He reached forward to unbuckle his dark-wash jeans and my back arched. Every second of additional waiting was *killing* me.

I wanted to tell him the view from where I hung was just as incredible. That the work of art I was now admiring from the perch he'd crafted for me was just as magnificent…but the length of satiny red cloth he'd tied across my mouth as a gag stopped me, so I just moaned instead, hoping the look in my eyes conveyed to him what my mouth couldn't say.

I watched without blinking as Blake removed every bit of his clothes until he was standing before me completely naked. His cock hard and standing proud. His deep gray eyes hungry. His pale skin like smooth, unblemished marble in some places, and covered in blackish-blue ink in others.

One day I would trace the lines of every tattoo. I'd inspect every bit of artwork he'd deemed worthy to grace his immortal body. One day—when he was ready.

Blake stalked forward, putting himself between my suspended knees. He ran his fingers up my stomach, and between my breasts until he was caressing my neck. He tugged the gag out of my mouth, and I licked my dry lips.

Looking deeply into my eyes, he latched onto some deep part of me. A part I normally kept buried—under lock and key. But he found it and he held me there. It was a quiet understanding. It was the dark parts of him calling out to the dark parts of me. As though meeting for the first time.

Recognizing their counterparts in another creature.

Blake dipped his head and kissed me softly, all the while his thumb was brushing small circles in my neck, making my body come alive with need. He slipped into my mouth and I moaned into him. He drank me in, his fangs skated over my tongue, so close to drawing blood.

He hissed as he pulled away, and I saw how his upper lip curled back—twitching as he tried to keep his more primal urges in check.

"Take it," I told him in a breathless voice as his cock brushed against my navel, sending a cascade of trembling warmth over the surface of my skin. "You have *all* of me," I told him again, wanting him to understand that I meant it.

He had my body. My soul. *My blood.* They were all his.

As I hoped he would be mine.

Blake considered my offer, his eyes flicking back and forth between mine, searching for any uncertainty. He wouldn't find it.

He slipped the gag back into place and knelt.

What was he—

My body stiffened as he found the vein on my inner thigh and bit down *hard* into my flesh. Pain and pleasure exploded through me all at once. I threw my head back at the explosion of sensation and moaned loud and long.

As Blake fed from me, his hand ran up the inside of my thigh, over the ropes and further up until his thumb brushed over my sex. I convulsed and he growled, his bite growing harder as his fingers found my opening and plunged inside.

I whimpered as my pussy clenched around him, my body straining at the binds holding me steadily in place for him. The venom of his bite made a sparkling fog settle over my mind and every flick of his fingers—ever circular press of his thumb against my clit had me on the verge of coming undone.

I almost cried out when his fangs slid out from my thigh. I was ready to beg him to take more, not even dizzy yet. His control was impressive.

But he surprised me yet again when he met my burning gaze for an instant before he gripped my opposite thigh with rough fingers and loosed an animal snarl before he bit down once more, doubling the dose of venom.

His fingers quickened their pace and just as I was on the cusp of finding my release he released my thigh and moved his mouth to my pussy, flicking his tongue over and over to coax me to a brutal orgasm that tore through my body like a bolt of lightning, leaving a lengthy sizzle in its wake.

Blake rose to his feet and met my eyes as he curled his hands around my hips. With a devilish grin, he pressed his cock against my opening, teasing me.

"Blake," I tried to moan around the length of cloth, begging him. "Please."

His grip tightened and he looked dead into my eyes as he said, "I'm going to fuck you hard and fast, and then just before your release, I'm going to bite you. Understand?"

My heart was pounding—my blood rushing in my ears. I nodded vehemently. *Oh, fuck yes…*

He pumped into me in one quick thrust, seating himself inside me all the way to the hilt. I bucked and groaned as my body adjusted to fit him, but he was already thrusting again. As my head lolled back to the front, I watched him watch me as he fucked me.

Blake's gaze never faltered as he took in my pleasure, making it his own. Every sigh, every moan, every shudder and twitch of my body—he drank it in and the heat in his burning black eyes only deepened.

He fucked me unlike anyone ever had before. No human had this amount of stamina. Only a vampire could fuck like this. With his venom still pumping in my veins and my body bound and gagged, I knew I would cum again fast—my body already clenching—the muscle straining and the quickening sensation in my womb rising to a crescendo.

Blake smiled as he watched the orgasm rise, my breaths quickening and my moans growing more frantic. Blake moaned with me and the sound of him so close to finding a release of his own tipped me over the edge.

He thrusted his cock into me three times more before I knew I couldn't contain it any longer.

I cried out and his fangs slid into my neck, the venom injected into my bloodstream intertwining with the orgasm in a way that had me literally screaming. Stars and dark spots danced in the corners of my vision and my core convulsed as the orgasm swelled within me until I could hardly breathe.

When it finally began to fade, my body sagged back against my binds and Blake released my neck, leaving a hot dribble of blood to roll down over my breast.

Blake hungrily lapped it up, pausing to circle his tongue around my nipple. His cock inside me was still rock hard and he had a smug look on his angelic face. "I'm not even close to finished with you," his whispered.

19

I awoke in Blake's bed, groggy and gloriously sore. In was the kind of deep ache that made you shiver as you stretched out your muscles. The unfurling of taut muscle its own kind of release.

I tried to remember how I'd ended up in the bed but couldn't quite grasp the memory. I'd been limp and utterly spent when Blake finally began to untie and unwind me from the ropes. Every brush of his fingers over my skin had sent shockwaves over my body—my skin so sensitive to the touch by the time he was through that I sucked in a breath each time.

He must've carried me to bed. I must've fallen straight to sleep.

The thin covers and sheets smelled as though they'd been freshly laundered with Blake's trademark clean linen scent. The notes of vanilla and suede soothing me to wakefulness. I yawned as I stretched out and felt around the bed for him, but my hands came up empty and cold.

"Blake," I whispered into the dark.

When no answer came, I slid from the bed and felt around in the dark for my clothes. I found the ropes easily enough, but my clothes were no longer beneath them on the floor. *Crap.*

I went back to the bed and tugged off the sheet, wrapping it around myself as though it were a sheath dress. It would have to do for now.

Padding out into the hall, I found the apartment quiet and dark. I hadn't the slightest clue what time it was, but I had to assume everyone was asleep. I cursed myself for passing out. I hadn't wanted to waste a minute of time with them, and now I'd probably slept through most of an entire day. *Damnit.*

I peeked into Frost's room, careful not to let the door handle make a sound as I turned it. I could just make out the burling shape of him atop his bed. The steady rise and fall of his chest told me he was out cold. I shut the door again, wincing as the tongue clicked back into the chamber.

There was only one other door in the hall besides the bathroom, and I had to assume that it was Ethan's room. I hadn't been in there yet. Careful to be quiet once more, I pushed open the door and found a lamp illuminating the space. The blankets on the bed were rumpled, but he wasn't there.

Pushing open the door the rest of the way I stepped inside, whispering his name. I peered around the door and found a long desk, filled with half-completed drawings and three more monitors, their screens a polished black. He wasn't in here.

I bit my bottom lip and continued into the living area, tucking the tail of the sheet in tighter to keep it from falling off. I found Blake dozing on the sofa, his arms crossed over his chest. With the soft light from the ignited fireplace casting an orange glow over his face he looked ethereal. But even in sleep his brows were slightly drawn, and his jaw seemed tense.

Where was Ethan?

I remembered he'd mentioned a back entrance to the tattoo shop. A way to get inside without leaving the building. Wandering back down the hall, I inspected the walls, looking for a door I may have missed. There was nothing.

The door to Ethan's room was still slightly ajar and I stepped back inside, finding what I had originally assumed was a closet on the right side of the room. I opened it and found a staircase instead, grinning.

A single fluorescent bulb illuminated the narrow staircase and I followed it down and to the right, and then down some more until I came out an open door and into a bright room. I shielded my eyes from the glaring light, squinting to make out the shapes and contraptions as my eyes adjusted.

"Rose?" Ethan said, spinning around on a short round stool. His caramel hair was disheveled, sticking up at an odd angle in the front. There was a smudge of something on the corner of his chin, and his eyes were bloodshot and wide as he took me in.

I looked at what he was so intently doing before I interrupted. The room was like a miniature lab. Like the one in the cave, but with some different equipment and a table of Bunsen burners and beakers, all lit with blue flame and bubbling.

He was inspecting something beneath the microscope in front of him. It looked like black ink.

What the hell was he doing?

"Ethan, have you been awake all night?"

He swallowed and moved his hand up to rub the spot of whatever-it-was from his jaw. "Is it that obvious?"

I bit back a grin and nodded. "A bit," I admitted. "But you're even more adorable when you have that gleam in your eyes."

His ears turned pink as I stepped closer and helped him get the smear of dried ink from his jaw. "There."

"Come here," he said suddenly, tugging me down to fall into his lap. I gasped in surprise as his hands came around my waist. He spun us back to the table and gestured to the microscope. "Go ahead," he told me animatedly. "Take a look."

I did as he said, pressing my eyes into the viewer and squinting to see through the illuminated backing of the sample glass thingy. With the light shining through the substance, I found it looked more like a very deep red color than black. But there were veins of black inside the liquid. *Moving* lines of black. Like living vines, they spread through the substance, slithering, retracting, and gyrating before my eyes.

I leaned back, puzzled. "What exactly am I looking at?"

Ethan grinned wide and planted a kiss on my forehead. "It's you," he said in a breath. "Well, a part of you. I took a few samples of your blood and marrow from the lab."

He must've seen the horror on my face because he hastily added, "Don't worry, I asked Azrael first. Did you really think I'd steal from a thousand-year-old vampire?"

Right. Ethan was a lot of things, but stupid *wasn't one of them.*

"So, what did you do with the samples?"

His ears turned pink again. "Well, I can't be sure without testing it, but I think I've synthesized a type of ink that would not only bind to vampire flesh but would allow the wearer to walk in sunlight."

"What?"

"I'm not certain yet—"

"You did it?" I squealed.

Ethan tipped his head, clearly uncomfortable with my praise. "It needs to be tested," he reminded me. "And even if it did work, it wouldn't be permanent. Just like a tattoo fades, the concentrated elixir I synthesized from your blood would also fade."

I took his face between my hands and forced him to look me in the eyes. "It's a start," I told him, smiling. "A really good fucking start."

Maybe with this Azrael could fill in the gaps. Figure out the rest of what was needed to make it permanent. Maybe soon, he wouldn't need me anymore…and I could be with my guys.

My heart swelled and a warmth spread over my body at the thought. I could have cried.

"All that's left to do now is test it," Ethan said, casting his gaze to the floor.

Wait…what? I'd been so excited; I'd forgotten about that part. "You don't mean…?"

He gave me a strained expression. "Who else?"

"No."

Ethan moved to rub my back. "If it doesn't work, then I'll only be burned. It'll hurt, but I'll heal."

"No."

He busted out the big guns in the form of a very stern Ethan look, complete with a hard gaze and the deepening of his voice. It didn't suit him. "Rose, I'm doing this whether you like it or not."

"Doing what?" A deep timbre asked, and Ethan and I spun to see Frost in the doorway, rubbing sleep out of his eyes.

Blake trailed behind him, squinting into the room. "What's going on? It sounded like a cat was being gutted."

I pursed my lips. I didn't squeal *that* loud.

I climbed from Ethan's lap and pointed at him accusingly. "Ethan here thinks he's found a way to make a vampire able to walk in sunlight using some scienced-up version of my blood and blood marrow..."

They looked between Ethan and I, aghast, slightly mortified, and more than a little stricken.

"I know," I said, drawing out the words. "Super awesome, right? But the idiot thinks I'm about to let him test it on *himself* and go walking out into the sunlight."

When I didn't get the immediate barrage of backup I'd anticipated, I snapped my fingers in front of their dumbstruck faces. "Hello," I said. "Anybody home. Did you hear what I said? A little backup would be—"

"I'll do it," Frost volunteered. "I'll test it."

I groaned. "That's not what I—"

"Me too," Blake intoned, stepping forward. "What do we need to do, Eth?"

"*Nobody* is going to test this. We have no idea what will happen," I stepped in front of them, blocking them from moving any further into the small laboratory.

Ethan made a strangled sound in his throat and I turned. "Do you have so little faith in me?" he asked, the disappointment clear in his expression.

I rolled my eyes. "Don't give me that face. *Of course,* I have faith in you, but this is—"

"It doesn't seem like you do." Frost crossed his arms over his chest and glared down the length of his nose at me. "If Ethan says he thinks he's done it —then he's probably done it."

"Yeah," Blake added. "Guy's a genius. Or did you forget that?"

Frustrated and near my boiling point, I clenched my fists and stepped back, gritting my teeth. They weren't playing fair. That isn't what I fucking meant, and they knew it. They were playing me. The glimmer in Frost's green eyes, and the ghost of a smirk on Blake's lips were a dead giveaway.

"Fine," I roared, throwing my hands up. "You want to risk it, then go right ahead. But don't come crying to me when you walk back in that door looking like burnt toast."

Smugly, Frost and Blake both snickered. Blake even tossed me a wink. Cheeky bastard.

"Now that we have permission," Frost said, his

voice dripping with sarcasm. "Tell us what we need to do."

Ethan rolled over to a tall metal shelf at the far end of the room and picked up a tattoo gun from the second tier. His steeped tea eyes flashed mischievously at Frost. "Looks like you're going to have to let me tattoo you, after all."

20

The smug look on Frost's face evaporated when Ethan explained to him what *exactly* he'd concocted. Turns out, having a best friend who was a tattoo artist—and an incredible one at that—wasn't enough to tempt Frost into getting any sort of ink.

Even Ethan had one tattoo. It was on the inside of his forearm—a simple runic symbol I didn't recognize. He admitted that he only had that single one because he'd needed to test out his vampire-healing-resistant ink. That and he wanted some practice on actual flesh before he would tattoo anyone. Practice skins were only so close to the real thing.

Unlike Blake, neither of them could think of anything they wanted to have on their bodies for… well, for their entire *immortal* lives. I got it. It was a big commitment. Who was to say they wouldn't get tired of looking at whatever they'd decided on two-hundred years prior?

I found a nail file in the bathroom and was grumbling to myself as I sat in the stairwell, filing my jagged nails back into their trademark sharp points. The black polish I usually kept on them was chipped and scratched and in dire need of replacement, but I supposed that would have to wait. I didn't think the guys kept that sort of thing lying around the apartment.

The sound of the tattoo gun humming downstairs kept me on edge. What if this didn't work? What if it had the opposite effect and they all burst into immediate flames? What if the ink they needled into their skin poisoned them somehow? What if it killed them?

And then, even more terrifying, what if it worked? What would that mean? For me?

For them?

For us?

My status as The Black Rose: a moderate threat against vampire kind would be instantaneously elevated to Rose Ward: the most coveted blood-bag in all the lands. If word spread about what my blood could do…

I shuddered.

It wasn't that I was worried about myself. I

could hide. And I'd always been damned good at running.

But the guys…

That wasn't a life I wanted for them.

I heard a deep laugh from down the stairs and listened as the humming sound cut off. I discarded the nail file and made my way back down, ready to play nice. The idiots obviously survived *getting* the ink laced with my blood needled into their skin, so that was promising.

They'd asked me to draw the heavy rolling curtains in the front of the shop earlier so Ethan could get at the rest of his equipment. I walked through the back room that they'd converted into a lab, and as I sauntered through the door leading out into the main shop, I found the three of them talking quietly as their gazes flicked back and forth to the windows.

I thought I heard Frost say something along the lines of, *maybe we should just open the door.*

Here we go, I thought.

This better fucking work.

"So, what'd you get?" I asked, crossing my arms over my chest—unable to keep the scowl from my face. When they were ready, I would open the curtains *a crack* and see what happened. They were nuts if they thought I was going to let any of them try to walk out the door into full sunlight.

It was three in the afternoon. The sun would be high in the sky and hot and *lethal*.

Three sets of eyes turned to meet my gaze. Ethan grinned. Blake smirked. And Frost still had that infuriating smug look on his face.

"Well?" I asked again, and Frost rose from the tattoo chair where he'd been sitting, shirtless, as Ethan worked on him. Ethan was removing his gloves and setting his equipment back into the gleaming stainless-steel caddy he had next to them.

His shop was even nicer inside than it looked outside. With industrial style beams and light fixtures set into the antique walls. Plush worn brown leather benches for seating and a matching tattoo chair. It was simple and yet distinguished. I wondered which of the guys did the decorating or if they'd hired out.

"Don't be mad," Ethan said preemptively.

I cocked my head as he stood and moved to stand next to Blake and Frost.

I narrowed my eyes at him. "Don't be mad about *what*?"

That was when I noticed what was tattooed onto Frost's left pec. And on the side of Blake's neck. On Ethan's opposite forearm.

They had all gotten the same design. It was a flower.

A rose.

A black rose in full bloom.

My mouth dropped open, but whatever I'd been about to say—whatever scolding remark—died in my throat. I swallowed past the lump there and pursed my lips to attempt to stop the traitorous tears from pricking at my eyes. My throat burned with the effort of keeping them at bay.

"Well that's…" I began, barely managing to keep the thickness from my voice. "Um…"

"See guys, I told you she wouldn't be mad," Blake said in his smoky voice, licking his lips as he turned back to me.

Mad? How could I be mad?

Out of anything they could've chosen, they'd decided that the one thing they'd all be comfortable with having on their bodies for the rest of their lives was something that would remind them of *me.*

My heart ached in my chest and when I finally found the air to breathe, I decided words wouldn't be enough and crossed the distance between us, folding myself into them.

Frost, Blake, and Ethan wrapped their arms around me. Someone planted a kiss on the top of my head. Someone's thumb was rubbing my shoulder. And a wide hand rubbed my back.

The scents of leather, vanilla, cloves, and Ethan's trademark nautical cologne enveloped me, bringing me a sense of peaceful calm I hadn't had since I was a kid.

"You *sure* you want to have to be reminded of

my annoying ass every day for the rest of forever," I choked, brushing the back of my hand over my eyes as they pulled away.

Blake shrugged.

Ethan offered me a small smile and nodded.

Frost made a joking face and ran a hand over his silvery hair. "Too late now," he said. "Looks like we're stuck with your annoying ass for good."

"So, are we doing this?" Blake asked after a beat of silence. "I'd rather get the pain over with quick in case it doesn't work. I don't know about you guys, but I don't want our Rose to have to play nanny to three burn victims for the rest of her visit."

He had a point.

"We open the blinds a crack," I said, gulping. "If you feel any pain at all, I'll drop them back down."

There really wasn't any need for anyone to get seriously hurt here. Tiny burns I could help them heal. I'd give each of them as much blood as I could spare. Make sure they got healed up fast.

"Okay," Ethan agreed. "That works."

Frost nodded his agreement. "Well, what are we waiting for? Let's get this barbecue going."

Ethan shook his head. It made me feel a bit better that out of all of us, Ethan seemed the calmest. He didn't seem worried about it not working at all.

Either he was putting on a brave face to show

confidence in his theory, or he really was that confident it would work. I prayed it was the latter as I stepped up to the window and took hold of the chain that, when pulled, would lift the heavy curtain.

Their faces grew hard as my fingers closed around the chain. Blake's jaw tightened, and a vein in Frost's neck grew to twice its usual thickness as he clenched his fists and his face reddened.

"Fuck Rose," Frost cursed. "Just do it."

I held my breath and lifted the curtain about ten inches.

They reeled back, hissing. I was about to drop it back down when I noticed the hissing had stopped, and though their fangs were out and their faces were strained, the bar of sunlight crossing over their nether regions didn't seem to be burning them. Good thing, or I'd have accidently barbecued three sausages.

"Shit," Frost cursed, frozen solid as he stared down at the patch of sunlight on his junk as though afraid to move and break the spell that was keeping his manly bits from being singed off.

"Um…" I let go of the chain. "Can the sunlight get you through your clothes normally?" I asked as I realized that none of them had bare skin exposed to the sunlight, just the top part of their jeans.

"No," Blake replied, slowly moving his bare hand down toward the light. "But the dispersion of the natural light should be at least singing us…" he trailed off. "Right Eth?"

Ethan nodded. "Yeah," he said, breathless as his mind worked to comprehend it all. His eyes unfocused and darting as he, too, lowered his hand toward the light.

I gritted my teeth as they all reached into the bar of sunlight as though they were willingly about to submerge their hands into a vat of acid.

I squinted my eyes closed, unable to watch, until I heard a deep bellowing laugh and opened them to find Frost with his green eyes wide and a smile on his face so wide it showed all his teeth. Ethan joined him in the laughing fit. Even Blake was smiling a real, *genuine* smile. Their skin wasn't burning.

It…*it worked…*

Well, fuck me sideways.

Unable to tear my gaze away, I watched as they played in the light, twisting their hands and wiggling their fingers.

In a flash of white blond hair and sinewy muscle, Frost was at my side. He lifted me, spinning me in a great big circle before he smooched me loudly on the lips and tore the curtain from the window, taking the whole cartridge system with it. He tossed it to the other end of the tattoo parlor, and it smashed into a shelf against the wall, knocking a bunch of pictures off to crash and shatter all over the floor.

I giggled as he bared himself to the light, puffing out his chest with a shit-eating grin on his usually grumpy face.

He was the proverbial bull in the china shop. But he was my bull, so I guess it was alright. I'd make him help Ethan clean up the mess later.

Blake and Ethan's eyes narrowed to slits as they shielded their eyes from the onslaught of sunlight, carefully making their way into the light, too. The four of us stood there, staring out into the street, up above the trees in the park across the street and into the clouds, where the mid-day sun was shining brightly in the summertime sky.

I noticed the strange stares of the shoppers as they passed by, curiously examining the sexy guys all standing awkwardly with wide grins in the window of the shop. I didn't think they noticed or cared.

I giggled again and wrapped an arm around Ethan's shoulders, leaning into him. "You really fucking did it," I said incredulously.

"Told you," he snickered.

My mind was exploding with possibility. My heart light as the aura of bliss from the guys washed over me. They didn't think they would ever see the sun again. Wouldn't ever feel its warm rays.

It was in part because of me that they now could. We didn't know how long it would last, or what other side-effects it may have, but for now, it was a victory. No matter how fleeting.

I noticed the hearse still parked across the street from the building. The driver sitting in the driver's seat with a glazed over look as he stared straight ahead. He hadn't even noticed our little spectacle. The surprise of realizing he'd probably been there the whole time, waiting for orders to return me to the cave, was short lived as I remembered what this meant.

"We have to tell Azrael," I said in a rush.

Ethan's smile faltered. "Do you think he'll finally let you go?"

"Only one way to find out."

21

The guys and I stepped out of the shop and into the afternoon sun.

"Fuck man," Blake said, shielding his eyes. "Your pasty ass is blinding."

He wasn't wrong. In the sun, Frost shone like a beacon. His usually tan skin had lightened considerably since he'd become a vampire. Making him look like a ghost of his former self. And shirtless as he was, I was surprised his paleness didn't blind oncoming drivers as we crossed the road.

"Speak for yourself," Frost grunted. "Goth bitch."

I chuckled.

Right again. In the sunlight with his pale skin, and dark hair and eyes, as well as the whorls of black ink etched into his skin, Blake did look sort of gothic. Like a prince of the underworld come to wreak havoc on earth.

Ethan was the only one who seemed unchanged. But then, with all the hours he spent in front of his computer, or with his nose in a book while we were young, being pale was just the norm for him.

"Hey," I said and knocked a knuckle against the window of the hearse to get the driver's attention. Nonplussed, he turned his glazed eyes on me and opened the door. Stepped out.

He didn't speak, just stared at me as though waiting for instruction. He didn't even show so much as a lick of shock at the fact that there were three vampires outside in broad daylight. The poor fucker had to be compelled to within an inch of his life.

"I need to get ahold of Azrael," I told him in a low voice as three older women strolled past, making no secret out of the fact that they were openly ogling my guys. They slowed as they passed, making it even more difficult for me to have this conversation without mortals overhearing it.

"…I'd butter him up and…" I overheard the snippet of conversation and a hot bolt of fury raced down my spine. I turned and sneered at them.

Finally noticing me standing there, they scowled back at me. I met each of their eyes in turn and told them without blinking, "Eyes to yourself, ladies. Didn't anyone ever tell you it's rude to stare?"

Without another word, they all blinked, my compulsion settling over them like a veil, and continued down the street.

"Did she just…?" I heard Ethan ask behind me, his words trailing off.

"Yeah. She did," Frost replied, and I didn't have to turn around to know he was grinning. I could hear it in the bastard's voice.

Get it together, Rose, I told myself, trying to settle the hot tremors of jealous rage from resurfacing. I was a bit embarrassed and maybe a little surprised at my knee-jerk reaction…but fuck it. I wasn't about to let anyone step foot into *my* territory. I just got them back, fuck if I would let anyone else try to get their grubby hands on them.

I shook it off and pursed my lips, turning my attention squarely back to the driver with my hands on my hips. Completely ignoring the guys jeering behind me. "Like I was saying," I almost shouted, trying to get the guys to shut up.

They did.

I huffed. "I need to get ahold of Azrael. Do you have any way to contact him?"

He didn't move.

"It's important," I added, hoping to find a snag in the compulsion Azrael had laid on him. Surely, he was thorough. Surely there were stipulations, like if… "It's a matter of my safety."

Immediately, the driver lifted a hand to his

inside breast pocket and drew out a phone. It was an old flip-phone. Black and nondescript.

I took it and the driver resumed his straight-backed stance.

Opening the phone, the screen powered on and I saw that the thing was even older than I thought. The screen was small and slightly pixelated.

Christ, someone was going to have to introduce Azrael to the 21st century.

Not it.

I pressed the arrow keys until I managed to get to the little green phone icon and eventually, to recent calls. There was a long list of only incoming call, all from the same unsaved number. It had to be him.

It was probably useless to ask the driver anything, so I put the highlighted bar over the number and hit *call.*

The guys drew in close around me, though none stepped into the shadow of the hearse. They were purposely keeping themselves in direct sunlight.

It was…cute.

The phone rang for so long I wasn't sure I was going to get an answer, but a second before I was about to hang up, the receiver picked up with a hollow click and a hard voice growled into the receiver. "What is it?"

It was Azrael alright.

"It's me."

"Rose?" His voice lost a bit of its ire.

"Yeah, listen, I need—"

"Has something happened?" He demanded. "Why are you calling, and how did you get access to this phone?"

"I would tell you why I'm calling if you would shut up for a second."

Silence, and then, "*Rose*," he growled.

I rolled my eyes. "I'm fine. Everything is fine. *Better* than fine, actually..." I trailed off, drawing out the suspense.

I could practically hear him frothing at the mouth on the other end. I might pay for this later, but for now I was reveling in it.

"I'm out here with the guys. We're catching some afternoon rays."

There was no response for a moment, and then I heard Azrael's intake of breath on the other end. "Show me," he bit out.

"He wants proof," I said, pulling the ancient cell from my ear. I fidgeted with the buttons until I found a really shitty camera and held it up to the three vampires standing next to the hearse. "Smile for the camera," I said cheerfully.

The picture was shit quality, but it would do the trick. Hoping Azrael wouldn't take Frost's brooding face, Ethan's scowl, or Blake's middle finger to heart, I clicked *send* and put the phone back to my ear.

Waited.

"Let me speak to Ethan," Azrael's hard voice came over the speaker.

My blood chilled at his tone and I glanced at Ethan, considering.

"*Now*," Azrael hissed.

I hesitated. "No," I replied, my tone sharp enough to cut stone.

"What did you just say to me?"

The guys were looking at me with expressions that told me I should stop fucking around with the thousand-year-old vampire and give him what he wants.

I turned my back to them, my heart beginning to thud loudly in my ears. "We'll cooperate, but on *our* terms. I want your word that they will not be harmed. *Ever.* And I want you to remove your compulsion from them."

"Anything else?" He barked.

I thought about it.

"I want that new truck you promised me…*and* I want to come and go as I fucking please from now on. I don't want to spend even a second more than I have to in that infernal *pit* you call home."

I held my breath.

"Is that all?" He drawled.

Was he…was he *laughing* at me? The nerve…

I was sure he could hear the grinding of my

teeth on the other end, but I didn't care. I wouldn't rise to the bait.

"I'll agree to your first three terms," he said, sounding almost bored. "The other is out of the question."

"I want—"

"*Rose,*" he warned again. "I will not argue with you. I don't need to. I could find you anywhere now. I have enough of your blood for my witch to do a thousand locator spells. And when I find you, I don't even need to drag you back. I don't need to fight you…"

I shivered as his words slithered into my ear canal and down into my chest, where a growing chill blossomed over my still-pounding heart.

"I could just compel you. Compel *them.* I could erase you from their minds in seconds," he paused. "So, dear Rose, I hope you understand that what I've just offered you is a gift and not a bribe. I don't do bribes. I don't do *negotiating.*"

"I—" I stammered, furious and disgusted and full of dread.

"Don't forget who you're playing with, pet."

"Don't call me that," I spat, unable to help myself.

A low laugh rumbled through the phone from the other end, and then Azrael's deadpan voice spoke again. "Now gather your things and get in the car—*all of you.* Judging by that photograph, you disregarded my request to remain within the building."

I tensed. *Crap.* It'd completely slipped my mind with all the excitement. Surely no one would be able to track me so quickly? Besides, it was broad daylight. We couldn't be attacked until after dark at least.

"You are no longer safe there…now would you mind passing the phone to Ethan?"

A tap on my shoulder had me jumping and spinning to find Ethan with his hand outstretched, a softness in his eyes that reassured me everything would be okay. *It's alright* he mouthed and nodded to the phone.

Wordlessly, I stuffed the phone into his hand and stomped back inside.

Fucking high-handed, cocky, power-crazed dickhead prick…

I'd show him. It might take some time, but one of these days, I was going to bring Azrael to his knees. And I was going to fucking enjoy it.

22

There was no way any of the guys were going to climb into the coffin, and I sure as hell wasn't about to volunteer. Instead, after grabbing my few things, a change of clothing each, and a vial of Ethan's ink and his tattooing equipment, we all piled into the hearse where we could.

Ethan and I sat up front with the driver, and Frost and Blake sat on either side of the coffin in the back, both of them watching the sun set from the windows along the way.

I wondered if Azrael's compulsion would make them forget where the cave was as soon as they tried to store the information. I could only imagine the migraine that would cause them. They weren't happy at all to learn they'd all been compelled to not be able to find me.

Frost was a bit relieved, though. He thought he

was going to go mad trying to figure it out, and now he knew why his mind wasn't able to connect any of the dots he tried to snag out of the dark. Soon, that compulsion would be removed, and they'd know where Azrael was keeping me. I had no doubt they'd want to stay as long as I did, but I had no way of knowing whether Azrael would allow that.

At least he'd agreed not to harm them…

I wasn't an idiot, though. Just because he agreed not to harm them himself, didn't mean he wouldn't compel someone else to do it. I knew how minds like his worked.

The last thing he told me echoed in my skull as the sun dipped below the horizon. '*You are no longer safe there…*'

Did that mean the guys wouldn't be safe there anymore, either? If someone was able to trace me to that location, what would happen to them if they returned without me to protect them?

I gulped hard, and noticing my tight expression, Ethan covered my fisted hand in my lap with his. "What is it?" he asked in a hushed tone.

What is it?

I could've laughed at the ridiculousness of the question, but I reined in the urge.

Let's see; we're at the whim and mercy of a thousand-year-old vampire while another, equally ancient and powerful hunts us down.

I couldn't believe I was thinking it, but without Azrael, would I already be dead?

Would *we* already be dead? I sighed. "The sun will set soon," I said, deciding to voice a separate worry from the one that was eating at me. "Without the witch's ward shielding me—"

"You're worried Raphael will be able to track you?"

I shrugged. "If Azrael has a witch in his employ, who's to say Raphael doesn't too?"

Ethan pursed his lips. "Fair point," he said. "But I think a witch would need something of yours. Like hair, or blood. or a personal belonging to find you. I doubt he would have any of that."

"How did you know who he was, anyway?" I asked. "You all seemed to know who Azrael and Raphael were before I did. You knew Raphael was the one who killed my mom. How long did you know?"

"That's a lot of questions."

I turned my attention back to the highway ahead of us. "I've got time," I joked. It was still another four hours to get back to the cave. We had nothing but time.

He chuckled and removed his hand from mine, following my gaze to the road. "Honestly?" he asked. "Everyone knows who they are. Well, every *vampire* does, anyway. We found out about them maybe a week or so after we changed. They're legends in the vampire world. In the whole of immortal society, really. The oldest and strongest of us."

I thought it strange that I'd never heard of them, but then again, I didn't really stop to chat with my victims. Even though at times I thought it may have been helpful to ask if they knew of a vamp with one eye brown and the other blue, it never seemed worth the risk of drawing out the kill. Besides, I didn't know the culprit was one of the most renowned vampires in the world. I thought he was just another undead bloke with a mean streak.

"Azrael was a big unknown," Ethan continued. "No one had heard from him in nearly a century until he came out of retirement about ten years ago."

When Raphael was compelled by my mother, my mind connected the dots for me.

"He caught wind that there was a mortal woman who'd compelled his brother."

"A pure-blood Vocari," I supplied. "Mom."

"Yes," Ethan replied, his eyes filling with sadness. "We don't know the whole story, but from what we were able to piece together, it sounds like Azrael tried to get Raphael on his side—explained to him what a pure-blooded Vocari could mean for their race. But Rafe didn't listen. If anything, it sounds like after he learned what Azrael told him—how the blood of a Vocari could have the potential to reverse the effects of the curse—he wanted your mother dead even more."

My brows drew together as my brain tried to chew all the new information. "But, why? Why wouldn't he want that, too?"

Another piece of the puzzle clicked into place as I remembered something else Azrael had said to the guys; '*this may come as a shock to you, especially if you're familiar with my dear brother's beliefs, but I do not relish what we have become.*'

And after that, when asked what he wanted with my blood; '*you might as well know*,' Azrael had said. '*For it's the same reason my brother wants to spill it.*'

"Two sides of the same coin," I whispered to myself before Ethan could respond. "One brother who hates what he's become, and another who relishes it."

Ethan nodded. "Rafe believes the curse of the sun and moon is a *gift.* As soon as he learned what Azrael wanted to do, he found your mother and killed her. Thought he killed you, too, successfully ending the line of the last Vocari."

"But he didn't."

"No," he said, bumping my shoulder with his. "And I'm damned glad of that…" he trailed off, his small smile fading and light brown eyes growing shadowed as he bowed his head. "But Rafael will stop at nothing to make sure Azrael doesn't succeed. He reveres the dark. They say he bathes in mortal blood and feasts on entire families in a single night."

My stomach turned.

"They say he keeps a harem of vampire concubines chained in his palace against their will, too—calls them his *wives*," Ethan grimaced, the disgust plain in the set of his sharp jaw. "He's named himself the unofficial king of darkness."

I huffed, my stomach roiling at his description of the monster as I spun the snowflake obsidian ring on my middle finger. "Sounds like he could use a good staking."

"I'd castrate him first," Ethan chimed in, surprising me with his vulgarity. I grinned up at him.

"Why hasn't anybody? Killed him, I mean?"

Ethan cocked his head at me, a crease between his brows.

"I mean, I get that the fucker is super strong and shit," I amended. "But if enough vamps banded together against him—"

"That's the thing," Ethan interrupted. "The vamps *do* band together. But they do it *with* him. Not against him."

"You think he compels them to join him?"

"Honestly," he replied with another heavy sigh. "I don't know. I would hope they weren't joining him of their own free will, but…"

He didn't have to say it. I'd come to realize that

Frost was right all those nights ago; not *all* vampires were total monsters. But there was more dark than light in the world of blood and fangs.

I may have killed a few who didn't wholly deserve it, but I had to believe deep down that I'd done more good than harm. Many of my victims had the reek of fresh blood on their breath before they met the business end of my metal stakes. And others had attacked first.

Licking my suddenly dry lips, I shook off the thoughts. I didn't want to think about it. "They might be," I finished for Ethan. "But what's his end game?"

That was the one thing I didn't understand. Why rally a compelled army to your cause if all you wanted to do was find and kill a single girl?

Frost turned to face me from behind the seat. His green eyes shone with flecks of gold that looked like sparks of fire in what remained of the dying light. "He wants to take over," he said. "We killed one of his lackey's not too long ago. The fucker was raving mad. Talking about how Rafe would lead us all into a new golden era of vampire."

...the fuck?

"He wants us all to bend the knee," Frost growled.

"And not just us," Blake added, not bothering to turn around. He ran a pale hand through his dark tousled locks. "Everyone."

I barked out a laugh. "You can't be serious. *Everyone?* Like all immortal kind? Shifters and witches and shit?"

Frost's hard glare didn't falter as he replied. "No, Rosie. Not just immortal kind."

I felt like I was going to be sick.

A sickening dread shocked my system and slithered over my skin. My lip curled back as I shoved the emotion aside in favor of one I could use. *Fury*. It'd been my companion for as long as I could remember.

When guilt weighed on me.

When heartache threatened to crush me.

When sorrow filled my bones with lead and scraped my throat raw.

Fury was there to pick me back up. It was there to lift my chin and breathe life back into my soul.

"I won't let that happen."

I didn't realize I'd said the words aloud until Ethan took my hand again, twining his fingers through mine. "*We*," he corrected. "*We* won't let that happen."

23

For the next thirty minutes or so, we were all quiet as night finally fell in earnest. All of us growing more tense with each passing minute.

"If they had the ability to track you," Ethan said, breaking the tepid silence while rubbing a circle in the back of my hand, "They'd have found you a long time ago."

I smirked. It wasn't *me* I was worried about, but I wasn't about to say that. I readjusted the stakes between my legs, making the holsters sit more forward so I could sit more comfortably.

"Why don't you just take them off?" Frost grunted. "There's still a lot of road to cover."

I bit the inside of my cheek, but only considered it for half a second. I was caught without my stakes once before and almost got a broken skull because of it—I wasn't about to make the same mistake twice. "No. I'm good."

Frost snickered, rolling his eyes.

A loud electric purring sound had both Ethan and I flinching. I was about to ask what it was when Blake pulled a phone out of his jeans and Ethan relaxed as he put it to his ear.

"Yeah," he barked into the device.

There was a pause before the atmosphere in the vehicle shifted. I couldn't quite make out what was being said on the other end of the receiver from where I was sitting, but Ethan and Frost sure could. A crease formed in Ethan's brow, and Frost looked like he was about to rip someone's head off.

"Speaker," Frost bellowed.

Blake pulled the phone from his ear and hit the button to put it on speakerphone.

"Get out of there," Blake told the caller.

"What do you want me to do?" A male voice asked on the other end. It wasn't anyone I recognized, and I struggled to understand what was going on that had them all so worked up.

"I want you to turn around and get the fuck *out of there*," Blake hissed. "It isn't safe."

"What's going on?" I whispered the question to Ethan. "Who is that?"

"Jerome," Ethan whispered back. "A client of mine."

"...they're torching everything, man," the guy on the other end said, his voice growing hard.

They're what?

Frost turned his steely green gaze on me. "They must've tracked you to the shop somehow," Frost explained in a brusque voice, his great big hands clenching into fists as his face reddened.

No...

"They're burning it down," Ethan added without emotion. "All of it."

Fire and ice warred for dominion in my chest. My breathing picked up and my hands curled into talons. This was *my* fault.

Hot, angry tears pricked at my eyes.

Blake gripped the phone tighter. "If it's who we think it is, you need to leave. *Now.*"

There was a gasp on the other end and all of us stiffened. "*Fuck,* man," the guy named Jerome cursed.

"*What?*" growled Frost.

"I see them," Jerome replied.

I stopped breathing.

"How many?" Ethan asked calmly.

"Six," Jerome replied, and listening carefully, I realized I could now hear the crack and hiss and *roar* of the fire somewhere nearby to where he was.

All their work...*their home*...maybe if the fire department got there fast enough it could be saved.

My fingernails dug deep half-moons into my palms.

The sounds of sirens sang out of the receiver and I sighed. Maybe if the building wasn't consumed yet. Maybe—

The sirens grew louder. Then came a scream.

The bloodcurdling sound gripped me, sending goosebumps over my skin and making my hair stand on end.

"What was that?" I demanded, loud enough for the caller to hear.

A second scream, this one male, joined the first. Then a third.

A fourth.

"What's happening?" Frost shouted into the received, snatching the phone out of Blake's stiff hand.

The vampire on the other end tripped over his words in his haste to speak. "They—they're…*oh fuck*…they're killing them. They're tearing them apart…"

My stomach turned and I gripped it, afraid I might be ill.

"Jerome *leave*," Ethan injected.

A hiss came over the receiver and then a clatter.

"Jerome?" Ethan asked, his face paling and tone growing higher in pitch with his panic.

There was the unmistakable sound of a scuffle. Then a deep *thud.* A sickening gurgle.

The line went dead.

My heart pounded against my chest. "We have to turn around."

"Not a fucking chance," Blake hissed, spinning to settle his black eyes on me. There was no space for argument in his tone, but I didn't fucking care.

My upper lip curled back, and I turned my attention to Frost and Ethan. "They're *killing* people," I shouted. "This is *not* an argument I'm going to have. We *are* going back."

An image of my mother, pale and unblinking in a pool of her own still-warm blood came unbidden to my mind and I gagged. *They were killing people.* The woman who'd screamed. She could've been someone's mother.

And the man—someone's father.

If we didn't stop them, nobody would.

They'd kill, and feed, and rape. Then they'd toss the bodies into the fire and compel anyone who saw to forget.

It'd happened before.

Fire's were a great way to get rid of immortal evidence.

Frost looked like he was about to blow his top, but he forced himself to draw in several deep breaths before he responded, meeting my venomous stare with a lethal one of his own. "She's right."

Blake glared at him with murderous intent, his fangs bared.

"Blake, stop," Ethan said, deadpan. "Rose *is* right. We can't allow them to keep killing. We have to try to stop them."

It was what they turned themselves for, wasn't it? To protect humanity? It was the same reason I trained for eight years to get to where I am now.

This was what we were bred for.

Our purpose.

I didn't want to put them in the line of fire any more than they wanted me in it. But I wouldn't sit here driving miss daisy while people were being slaughtered.

How could I?

How could *they?*

"There's only six of them," I tried to make Blake see reason.

"We don't know how old they are."

"I've killed four by myself at once," I told him. "We can do this."

Surprise flickered over his sharp-angled features before his face settled back into a hard mask. "What if he's there?"

My jaw clenched. I knew none of us were a match for Raphael. But together…

Maybe.

It was a risk we'd have to take.

"*We end him.*"

Ethan bowed his head.

Frost suddenly couldn't look at me.

"Yeah," Blake said, his voice dripping sarcasm while a deep unease crept into his stare. "Or we all die trying."

I turned to the driver, grabbing his arm to get his attention. He was driving along as though nothing had happened. His face serene as the tires continued to chew pavement, taking us in the opposite direction of where we needed to go.

"Turn around," I demanded.

He didn't respond. I laced my voice with compulsion and jerked his head to face me. "*Turn around.*"

"I can not divert from the route," he replied robotically.

Useless.

I jerked the wheel from his hands and before he could fight me for control, I drew a stake and butted him hard on the back of his head. He slumped in the seat and his foot dropped heavily onto the gas pedal. The old hearse roared down the highway and I had to swerve to avoid hitting a minivan with six little people stickers on the back window.

Vaguely, I was aware the guys were cursing and shouting, but I almost had it. I managed to lift his leg from the gas pedal and snake my foot down between his legs to get to the brake. We bounced onto the gravel at the side of the road and into a field, the tired chewing dirt and tall grass before we skidded to a sudden, jarring stop.

Horns honked in our wake and Frost groaned as he held the top of his head. He must've hit it on the roof when we'd bounced off the highway.

I threw the hearse into park and nudged Ethan to get out so I could go around to the drivers' side.

"Too slow," he said, but obligingly got out of the way so I could stand outside next to the vehicle. "We need to run."

The back hatch clanked open and Frost and Blake were outside with us in an instant.

"You're the fastest," Ethan said to Frost. "You'll have to carry her."

What?

It took a second for my brain to catch up. The drive back would take me an hour at least—and that was if I was breaking *a lot* of traffic laws. But vampires are *fast*. We could cover the distance back to Baton Rouge in ten minutes. Maybe less if they really pushed it.

Speed was something else that developed with immortal age.

I shook my head. What had I been thinking? An hour return trip would make the whole thing futile. By then they'd be done and gone. Hundreds killed. The building reduced to ash and beam.

"What is that?" Blake asked suddenly, and I strained my ears to hear what he was referring to. It was a ringing.

The driver's cellphone.

There was only one person who would be calling. I ignored the sound, stomping around back to grab my bag. I unzipped it and drew out my Katana, strapping it across my back. I stooped to make sure the laces of my combat boots were tied tightly and drew my hair back into a ponytail with a stray elastic I found at the bottom of my bag.

"Let's move," I said, my blood buzzing with anticipation of the oncoming battle. I'd been dying for this for days now. Hungry for blood. I *ached* for those who'd already lost their lives, but I lusted after their killers. I was going to fucking *enjoy* this. As I made my way to Frost, I heard the phone go off again.

I ground my teeth. "Leave the vial of ink with the driver," I told Ethan and watched his face crumple at the suggestion. I had to be realistic, we may not make it back. But if there was a cure for vampirism hidden somewhere in my genetic makeup, then it was my duty to make sure it got into the *right* hands. Ethan's vamp sunblock ink could steer Azrael in the right direction.

Don't even get me started on why all of a sudden, I was thinking of the *right hands* as being Azrael's…

Better than his savage brother, though.

Ethan nodded tightly and turned back to the hearse.

Frost lifted me into his arms as though I weighed

no more than a babe. He cradled me against his warm, hard chest and locked his fingers just above my hips.

"I'll take point when we get there," I told him. "You'll all be needing a minute to catch your breath."

His jaw twitched. He didn't agree, but he didn't disagree, either.

It would have to do.

"*Well*," I said, exasperated. "What are you waiting for? Giddy up!"

24

I had to tuck my face in tightly to Frost's chest as he ran. Have you ever gone two-hundred miles an hour without protection from the wind? If I so much as tried to open my eyes, they instantly watered and burned. And I didn't think the deafening sound of wind rushing into my ears would ever fully fade.

As Frost slowed and I was finally able to turn my head out from the shelter of his wide chest and open my eyes, I gasped. We were still several miles away. Skating down empty streets and abandoned alleyways to avoid someone catching sight of us. But the billowing smoke pouring into the otherwise clear night sky was unmistakable.

My chest tightened and I glanced up to see Frost's jaw twitch as we drew nearer. "Put me down," I told him as he skirted around a bank of parked cars and hopped a fence in a single bound, landing us on our feet at the edge of the huge park that stood across from their building. He did, setting me gently down while keeping a hand on my arm to steady me.

His barrel chest was heaving hard as he drew in exerted breaths through his nostrils. I regained my footing and stretched out my stiff muscles, drawing my stakes. Through the trees we could see snippets of the beautiful old concrete corner building where Ethan's shop and their apartment were. But now the light-colored walls were charred black. Now, smoke and flames billowed from the windows.

Now, it was too late to save it.

I turned to Frost just as Ethan and Blake sped into the park, skidding to a stand-still beside us.

"I'm so sorry," I managed, my voice hard, but cracking.

Blake's eyes flashed with murder. "It's not your fault."

But it was…

A scream ricocheted into the night and spurred us all back into action. They were still attacking. We might've been too late to stop the fire, but we weren't too late to stop the carnage.

A fire engine squatted against the sidewalk just on the other side of the trees, vacant. As we ran nearer, at a slightly quicker than normal pace that I could match, I began to notice what the strange light-reflecting bits scattered on the sidewalk and the road were…

Body parts.

Fireman body parts.

A helmeted head there. A leg and arm bent at odd angles next to it. Blood spattered blacktop reflecting flames in crimson.

My stomach lurched.

Ethan's fangs slid out and his jaw worked to contain his thirst in the presence of so much fresh blood.

Frost and Blake looked pained, too, but not nearly as affected.

I supposed my blood only worked to stave off the cravings if people's blood stayed *inside* their bodies. Not even a properly sated vampire could resist a king's buffet.

A twig snap alerted me to someone approaching and I squinted into the foliage to see the vague shapes of people as they drew nearer the burning building. "Ethan," I said, getting his attention. "Keep the people away."

He narrowed his eyes at me. "But—"

"Please," I said, interrupting him. "Just keep them back."

His lips tightened, but he nodded.

Then I was running, Blake and Frost flanking me left and right. It was time to stake some motherfuckers.

The thrill of the hunt sharpened my focus. Lengthened my strides. My blood sang with the adrenaline rush and despite myself, I smiled.

They wanted The Black Rose.

Come and fucking get her…

I plowed into the first vampire I saw. A tall, lanky fucker with greasy brown hair and a gaunt face. He was drinking from a news-reporter's carotid, and by the look of the scene around him, he'd already finished with the rest of the news crew.

He lifted his head and his bloodlust hazed blue eyes met mine. He wasn't anticipating an attack. The fucker barely had time to drop his fresh kill and move into a fighting stance before I was on top of him. I dodged his right hook and snaked my right leg out to swipe his from under him. He landed hard on the blood-soaked pavement, dazed for the fraction of a second I needed to stake him.

The metal tip burrowed through flesh and muscle, *cracked* through rib bones and found its mark. His gaunt face slackened, and he choked as though the stake had perforated his windpipe instead of his heart. A dribble of blood rolled over his bottom lip, and then he was gone. His blue eyes losing focus as death took him.

I freed the stake from his chest and roared, my inner lioness baring its feral teeth, my limbs lithe and light as I surveyed my surroundings, searching for my next kill.

Blake was on the roof of the building next to their burning one. I glanced up at the exact moment he tore an arm off the vampire he was fighting. The high pitched mewl so loud it rose above the roar of the flame.

That's my boy.

Even though I was still at the other side of the street, I could feel the waves of suffocating heat rolling off the structure. Inside, it looked like the mouth of a volcano, *or the seventh circle of hell.* The heat so intense and the flames so strong they all blended together into a rippling, waving, bright orange glow.

Sweat slicked my palms and beaded on my fore-head. I couldn't see Frost or Ethan anywhere. Where were they? Where were the rest of the vampires?

Just as I thought it, my amber eyes latched onto another. He was frozen like a deer in the headlights. He clutched a severed arm in his blood-coated hands and from his stance near the building and the mass of corpses at his feet, he was the unlucky bastard tasked with getting rid of the evidence. He was clearly tossing the bits of deceased human into the fire.

I didn't have time to allow the rising emotions at the sight of so many dead humans—to feel grief stricken for all the families that'd just been broken...

Instead, I did what I do best; I let fury eat up the pain and turn it into fuel for the fight.

Got you, fucker.

I charged, a battle cry tearing from my aching lungs. The vampire's eyes widened, but unlike the other, he was ready for me. He saw me coming and he lifted a crowbar from the ground, snarling as I descended upon him.

He lashed out with the bar, missing me by a hair as I thrusted my stake in, aiming to incapacitate. The vampire was faster, dodging my advance and parrying to the right. He lunged again, hissing, and I whirled out of the way. But he anticipated that, too, and landed a blow with the back of his hand across my face.

Blackness flashed in my vision and I shook my head as I lifted it, tasting blood on my tongue. I laughed.

Damn, how I'd missed this. My skin crackled with energy as I lifted my head to meet his gaze and he watched me, horrified at my bloody smile. At how I laughed in his face. He moved to attack again, and I spun out of his reach, staking him in his kidney from the back.

Awe, the darkness whispered in my mind. *I thought he would actually give me a challenge…*

Too bad.

The vampire drew in a broken breath, and his millisecond of pause was all I needed to finish the job. In a single movement, I sheathed the stake from my right hand in its holster and lifted it to the hilt of my Katana. Widening my stance, I drew the blade and swung in one long, beautiful arc of shining steel and spraying blood.

His head bounced to the ground and I punted it into the flames as the rest of his body slumped.

I wiped his spatter from my cheek, probably just smudging it, and scanned for the next one, finding Frost instead. He had just finished dispensing with one in the tree-line, and he was watching me, his lips parted and bright green eyes wide with something between horror and awe.

I was just as impressed with them, though, and I beamed as I took in the strong lines of him. *Fuck,* it was like they were born for this.

The vampires here weren't very old, that much I could tell, but they were certainly older than my guys…

Rule number one in a fight, don't check out your fellow comrades. I was so enamored watching Frost that I didn't see or hear the other fucker coming until he was practically on top of me. He hit me hard in the back and I flew several feet toward the flaming building before I landed in a breathless heap on the ground and he was digging his knee into my back. My Katana and the stake from my left hand clattered to the ground ten feet away and rolled beneath the fire truck.

Fuck.

My breath came back after a heartbeat and I kicked up my left leg, nailing the bloodsucker somewhere in the back with my stiletto heel.

It was enough for me to be able to buck him off and roll into a crouch.

I heard a distinctive grunt that had me breaking focus for a fraction of a second to see that a group of three had surrounded Frost.

What the fuck? I thought there were only six?

Obviously more had come to join the blood bath.

"Ethan!" I called, blocking a blow from the vamp and feinting to the left as he went right. I jumped to my feet and nailed a good, hard kick to his abdomen. "Blake!"

Someone needed to help Frost. He wouldn't be able to take three at once.

I was distracted and unable to keep focus as the vampire cursed and retaliated with a kick of his own. The air *whooshed* from my lungs and I strained to get it back, hunched over and sputtering.

A knee came up and before I could block, it slammed into my face. A throbbing pressure built behind my eyes and dark stars danced in my vision. A gush of blood rushed from my nose and I choked on the hot, metallic taste, coughing as I struggled to shake off the stun.

The vampire had his hand reeled back to strike,

his long fangs bared and brown eyes wild. This time, I was faster, I ducked and rolled, coming up on all fours a few feet away before I lunged for his throat. I dragged my sharp nails over his jugular, effectively tearing out his throat. My fingers slipped over the polished metal stake as I drew it from its holster—my last available weapon before I would need to start getting really fucking creative.

As the poor bastard clawed at his ragged neck, I rammed it into his chest. I didn't wait to make sure he was dead, I withdrew the bit of metal and whirled, ready to go to Frost's aid, my muscle burning with the urge to run.

Instead I was face to face with another vampire. This one tall and broad. I shivered as that otherworldly feeling clawed up my spine and made my insides tremble. With the flames to his back, his face was cast in shadow, but I recognized that long hair, pulled back in the style he always wore it. I saw the flicker of firelight cross his brown eye, turning it blazing amber before it lit his blue one with flecks of gold.

"That's quite enough, I think," he said and there was a note of something in his voice I hadn't heard before.

"Azrael—" I began, but the vampire *tsked* me and I craned my neck back to get a better look at him, my stomach dropping to my toes.

Raphael shook his head. "I'm afraid not."

I tore my eyes from his and without missing a beat, I struck out, trying and failing to catch him by surprise.

He caught my arm mid-strike, jarring me to a rough stop before he *crushed* the bones in my arm, forcing me to drop the stake. I cried out as splintering agony scattered through my nerve-endings like buckshot. My stomach roiled and I clenched my jaw to keep my head.

When he let go, I clutched my arm to my chest, breaths sawing in and out through the tiny gaps in my clenched teeth. A high pitched sound assaulted my ears and it took me a moment to realize the sound was coming from me.

Raphael grinned down at me, his fangs flashing in the orange glow. "A valiant effort, Miss. Ward, but I'm afraid your skills are of no use here."

I backed away a step, then another. He advanced slowly, enjoying himself. Taking his time.

This kind of monster liked to play with his food, I realized. If I could just keep him talking, maybe I could…

"It's no use," he chuckled, the sound throaty, with a bass-like tempo that I could feel reverberating in my chest.

Fuck, I forgot he could read my thoughts. *Damn.*

I was even more fucked than I thought.

Raphael nodded as though agreeing with me,

still advancing as I backed towards the fire truck still fifteen feet away. If I could…

I stopped the thought, trying to conceal it from him.

"Why don't you just give up now and save us both some time. *Save yourself* some hurt pride, hmmm?" he crooned.

What?

As I backed towards the fire truck and away from the scorching heat of the burning building in front of me, I saw Blake atop the roof. He was just as bad off as Frost was. There were two attacking him. One landed a hard hit to his ribs and I saw him buckle from it. A third blood sucker was scaling the wall at the opposite end of the street, going to join the fight.

Frost was barely hanging on. His ankle was bent at an odd angle and he limped as he fought—keeping the three still attacking him back, but not without what looked to be a huge amount of effort and strain. He'd clearly already sustained several injuries. He wouldn't last much longer.

My throat closed and a hard ball formed in my chest, crushing my lungs and gripping my heart. *No.*

No. This wasn't happening. I was shaking my head, over and over as I moved, my arm throbbing now. Head pounding.

Not my guys.

Not here. Not now. I couldn't watch this.

I should have known there were more than six. That more would come.

I shouldn't have been so cocky. I should have been more careful.

When Blake said Raphael himself could be here, I should have believed him. I shouldn't have dismissed it.

He already took my mother from me. He couldn't take my guys, too. He…

I…I…

A powerful sob racked my body and my eyes stung.

It's my fault.

My fault.

"I can make it stop," Raphael said, his eyes slitted. His words might as well have been a siren's lure. I froze, my heart in my throat. The vampire held out his hand. A hand that looked so like his brother's. He looked at me with eyes that could have been Azrael's too, if it weren't for the malevolent gleam that made them seem brighter. Sharper.

Like he was imagining a million ways to break me and enjoying the horror picture show his mind concocted.

Crazed, my mind supplied. He looked like a fucking psychopath.

Raphael frowned, and his heavily lidded eyes deepened in shadow.

Oh shit. He didn't like that…

"Kill me then," I bit out, abandoning my goal of making it to the truck and my weapons that were safely tucked from view beneath the rear. "Call off your dogs and let them go and I'll surrender."

Raphael's shoulders vibrated with silent laughter. "Kill you?" he said, pausing to catch his breath before laughing audibly. "Oh, you stupid girl…"

He must've seen the question in my stare because he stopped laughing as suddenly as he started and halted in his advance. Stopping a mere two feet away. Close enough that he could reach out and grab me and I wouldn't be able to see it coming. I gulped. "Killing you wouldn't be any fun," he taunted. "I have much more…*interesting* plans for you, my Black Rose."

Raphael reached out a hand toward my face and I recoiled. He surged forward and grabbed my face. His sharp nails bit into my cheeks and I saw a flash of wild eyes before his lips closed over mine, stealing a rough kiss. The smell of expensive cologne clogged my nose, laced with something putrid. Rotting. Like overripe apples left out in the sun. His tongue skimmed my lower lip and I tasted blood.

I almost barfed into his mouth and managed to break free with a perfectly placed knee to his groin. But though it made him tear his lips from mine, he didn't budge. Anger, fevered and unrestrained, boiled in his haughty stare.

White spots burst in my vision as my head snapped back. My mouth filled with blood and I fell, landing in a heap on the pavement, the jarring movement jostling my broken arm in a way that made me hiss in pain.

I blinked into focus to find him staring down on me with disgust. "On second thought," he said, wiping the blood from his knuckles with a kerchief. "I think I *will* kill them all. I'm not very fond of loose ends."

I noticed one of the vampires taking turns attacking Frost was glancing back toward Raphael.

Rafe nodded and I pushed myself up, trying to find my voice—to scream. To warn him. To warn them all.

The fucker was toying with them. His lackeys didn't have orders to kill yet. Just to distract. My guys could hold their own, but who was I kidding? They couldn't stand up against three vamps each. Three vamps older and stronger than they were.

It just wasn't possible.

"Frost," I croaked, unable to see more than vague shapes after Raphael's hit. My vision was blurred and stained with pockets of light and dark that I couldn't blink away.

"Come now," Raphael said with a saccharine tenderness, making me shiver. "It's time to go."

His hand closed around my upper arm and I

suddenly found my voice. The shooting pains demanding a vocal release. I screamed.

A white blond head turned.

A blow was stuck.

Frost fell.

Shadowed shapes fell upon him in a wave of black.

I blinked as Raphael lifted me, my vision clearing to find Ethan speeding out of the trees. He'd been searching for the source of the scream, his head snapping back and forth. But he saw Frost instead, and I watched as he tore one of the vampires off his friend, then another. Throwing them as though they were rag dolls, into the trees of the park.

"Run," I tried, but my voice was hoarse and brittle. The scream had done something to my vocal cords, and I could do little more than wheeze and squawk. "Get…away…"

A loud bellow sounded over the roaring of fire and I looked up in time to see the shape of a body falling from the building. It was Blake.

I knew it. I could *feel* it.

Had he jumped? Or was he…?

I couldn't finish the thought. I just wanted this all to be over. I wanted the hurt to stop. The fury was fading, unable to keep up with the building emotions of heartbreak and despair vying for dominion over my soul.

I knew right then that whatever Raphael planned to do to me, it couldn't possibly hurt me more than this. Nothing could ever compare to the helplessness I felt *right now*. At the knowledge that I alone had led my guys to their deaths.

That without me, they would be alive and whole somewhere. Living their lives unaware of the evil lurking in the shadows.

I wished…

Another sob bloomed in my chest.

I wished they'd never met me.

Raphael stiffened and his hand that was holding tight to me like an iron manacle, loosened. I slipped from his grasp and yelped as I fell back onto the ground, landing on my injured arm.

"Brother," the deep voice filtered through the cacophony of sound and I struggled to squint into the haze down the street to see him. Azrael's thick-soled boots crunched over broken glass and debris. His wide frame blotted out the light as he neared.

"It's been a while," was Raphael's response. He was trying for nonchalance, but even I could hear the note of surprise in his tone. He hadn't anticipated this.

I sure as fuck didn't, either. My mind raced to make sense of it.

As the two oldest vampires in the world had their fucking moment. The stare down of all stare downs, I searched for Ethan and Frost, having a feeling in my gut…

Ethan knelt next to a hunched form that could only be Frost. His back was to me, but by the relief on Ethan's face, I knew he was still alive, if barely.

I found something else in his face, too, as he, too, turned his attention to Azrael's approach. He wasn't surprised. Another wave of relief flooded his gaze and the pieces clicked into place. I'd sent him back to leave the vial with Azrael's driver. The phone had been ringing.

He…he'd *told Azrael* where we were going.

Ballsy fucking move.

I didn't know whether to kiss Ethan or smack him. If we all survived this, though, I was hoping to get to do both. Definitely more of the former.

Without warning, Raphael vanished from my side. I thought for an instant that he fled, but a *clap* of thunder shook the ground and I realized he was attacking. And the sound of their bodies colliding was like a hammer hitting stone.

Ethan found me amid the carnage and moved to stand, his face paling. I shook my head and pointed with my uninjured hand. "Blake," I managed, my voice sounding like I'd been gargling rocks. I pointed to the edge of the building, where the other vampires were jumping down, presumably to finish him off, if he wasn't dead already.

Ethan hesitated and I ground my teeth, making

sure it was conveyed in my stare that if he came to me over helping Blake that I wouldn't forgive him.

He let loose an uncharacteristic growl and bolted for the building and Blake.

Relief flooded my senses and I pulled my aching form towards the fire truck. I had to be ready in case Azrael didn't win the fight. I had to…

My mind was growing foggy, and when I blinked, the black spots grew, taking longer to disperse than they had been a moment before. My right eye was throbbing, and a red substance was stinging it, making it more difficult to see.

I sagged only five feet away from the glint of steel just behind the rear tire of the fire engine, leaning my head against my bicep to catch my breath. With unfocused eyes, I was powerless to move as I watched the dance of immortal kings in the streets of Baton Rouge.

Maybe wrong place, wrong time, but I couldn't help thinking how many people were going to have to be compelled after this monumental fuck-up.

Azrael and Raphael were nothing more than dark shapes blinking into and out of focus. The sounds of their epic fight so loud they physically hurt my ear drums.

I winced at each *booming* hit.

Please, I thought to myself, sending up a silent plea. *Please let the guys get out of here. No matter what. They have to live.*

Please let them all live.

And then the darker part whispered *and let Azrael tear that motherfucker's black heart from his rotted chest.*

I squinted past the fight, finding movement further away in the haze. The silhouettes of seven —*no nine*—bodies grew in size as they neared. I thought they were humans and attempted to move again, needing to get up and help them. Tell them to stay back. I managed to crawl on my belly to the tire of the truck and reach a shaking hand beneath, trying without success to reach the hilt of my Katana.

But it wasn't humans.

That tickle of otherness slunk down my spine and filled my gut with dread. They were vampires.

Raphael noticed them, too. He landed an earth-shattering kick into Azrael's chest, sending his brother spiraling through the air to land among the oncoming crowd of vamps.

No…

As Azrael stood, I half expected the vampires to jump him. It would be a damned bloodbath. Surely even Azrael would have a hell of time fending off *nine* vampires at once. My fingertips brushed the smooth black grip, but I couldn't quite get my hand around the hilt. Grunting, I pressed my face against the hot rubber of the tire to get a better angle, reaching across sharp bits of glass and debris.

My hand closed over the hilt just as a hand

closed over my ankle, viciously dragging me over the debris. My skin scraped raw over the rubble. I lashed out, swinging the blade blindly. A sickening thud preceded an animal hiss and the blade was torn from my grasp.

Raphael was clutching a bloodied stump to his chest, staring down at his severed appendage in horror.

"*Leave*," the word was a brutal snarl torn from the chest of Azrael as he approached once more, this time flanked by nine vampires.

They're with him.

I could have laughed.

I wanted to sing.

Oh, *hell* yes. Kill the fucker.

"Go back to the hole you crawled out of and stay there," Azrael barked, the challenge in his tone plain as his eyes bore into his brothers. "If I ever see your face again, brother, I *will* end you."

Wait…he wasn't going to kill him?

"Fucking kill him," I tried to say, but the words came out slurred and not making any logical sense as I intended them. My vision blurred again, and my head was suddenly too heavy to hold up anymore.

Raphael's blow to my temple must've really fucked some shit up in there. My right eye still throbbed and my vision in it was narrowing to a pinprick.

My good hand clawed at the pavement, trying to drag myself to where Raphael had discarded my Katana.

Fine, I thought, *if Azrael wouldn't kill him,* I *would.*

"Rose," his soft voice brushed over my face. His fingers lightly touched a tender spot on my temple.

My head lolled back, and I found Azrael staring down at me. After the initial flinch of fear that it could be Raphael, I realized it *was* actually quite simple to tell the difference.

They were both fucking nuts, but Azrael didn't have so much of that untethered insanity in his eyes as his brother. And his hair was longer, I thought.

I searched immediately for Raphael, confused as to why I was staring into the eyes of Azrael when his psychotic twin was just there a second ago. I craned my neck to survey the entire street but came up empty-handed. He was…gone.

Fury sizzled back into my chest and I growled. "Why…why let fuck away get…"

I knew I wasn't making sense, but I couldn't seem to connect what my mind was thinking and what my mouth was trying to say.

I cried out as Azrael lifted me from the ground, cradling me against his bare chest and what was left of the shirt he'd been wearing, shredded to scraps from the fight. But there wasn't a mark on him. He'd already healed any injuries he may have had.

Beneath the torn fabric was smooth, unblemished muscle. Warm and hard.

I tucked my shattered arm carefully into my chest and tried to fight his hold, but it was no use. I was utterly spent, and whatever was wrong with my head was making it unfairly hard to do anything.

"Clean up this mess," Azrael barked at the group of vampires still standing protectively around him. "Leave no evidence."

They vanished to carry out his orders. He stopped one of them with a look and added, as what I assumed was an afterthought. "There are three vampires with us. They aren't to be harmed. See that they're tended to and then bring them to me."

My heart beat out a discordant rhythm. They were alright? Was he certain?

His gaze lowered to rest on my battered face, looking at me with incredulity. As though he was only just seeing me for the very first time. His brows lowered as he studied me, seemingly perplexed. "I can hear their thoughts," he said in a low whisper, his chest rumbling against my side in a way that somehow soothed me almost as much as those five beautiful words.

My body sagged against him and I was able to draw a full breath, my chin quivering as the reality of what almost happened settled into my core.

But it didn't, another part whispered. *They're alive.*

We are all alive.

Except…

I licked my lips and croaked. "You…stupid…"

I'd meant the insult to be a revelation of verbal assault, but again my mouth wasn't listening to my brain. "Should killed him…"

His brows drew together in worry and a muscle in his jaw twitched. "You should stop talking, Rose. We need to get you help."

His hold on me tightened.

My eyes crossed and I knew I was dangerously close to passing out, but I needed him to know first. I needed him to know that though I would be eternally grateful to him for saving my guys, he was the worst kind of idiot.

He had the fucker in the palm of his hand, and he *let him go…*

If I learned anything from the one vampire I'd ever let get away, it was that they *always* came back to bite you in the ass.

"Stupid fuckermother." I grumbled.

Azrael smirked. "Yes," he breathed, the smirk fading as he adjusted me in his arms and began to walk away from the flames and smoke. "You might be right."

Continue Rose's story in REDEEM ME, The Last Vocari, Book 3!

Get it on Amazon!

Printed in Great Britain
by Amazon

19706567R00154